The Power of Your Subconscious Mind

Unleash Hidden Mind Forces — Reprogram Thoughts for Health, Wealth & Limitless Success

A Modern Translation

Adapted for the Contemporary Reader

Thomas Troward

Translated by Tim Zengerink

Table of Contents

Preface Message to the Reader...1

Introduction 2

I: The Hidden Power...7

II: The Perversion Of Truth..37

III: The "I Am" 49

IV: Affirmative Power..52

V: Submission 55

VI: Completeness...60

VII: The Principle of Guidance 64

VIII: Desire as the Driving Force..67

IX: Touching Lightly 72

X: Present Truth..75

XI: Yourself 77

XII: Religious Opinions 81

XIII: A Lesson from Browning 87

XIV: The Spirit of Opulence..90

XV: Beauty 93

XVI: Separation and Unity 98

XVII: Externalisation 106

XVIII: Entering into the Spirit of It...................................110

XIX: The Bible and the New Thought.................................115

XX: Jachin and Boaz 144

XXI: Hephzibah... 148

XXII: Mind and Hand 153

XXIII: The Central Control 156

XXIV: What Is Higher Thought?...................................... 159

Thank You For Reading 161

Preface
Message to the Reader

Rebuilding the Greatest Library in Human History

Thousands of years ago, the Library of Alexandria was the heart of global knowledge — a sanctuary where the wisdom of every known civilization was gathered and shared freely.

And then, it was lost.

Now, we're rebuilding it — and you are invited to join us.

At the Library of Alexandria, we've set out to make every book available to every person on Earth — not just in print, but in every language, every format, and for every reader.

Here's how we do it:

- **Deluxe Print Editions at True Printing Cost** - Order any book as a high-quality paperback, elegant hardcover, or stunning boxset — and only pay what it costs to print. No markups. No middlemen.
- **Unlimited Access to the Greatest Works** - Enjoy thousands of timeless classics — from Plato to Shakespeare to Tolstoy — in beautiful, modern eBook and audiobook editions. Read and listen without limits — for every reader, everywhere.
- **Modern Translations for Every Language & Dialect** - We're reimagining the classics in clear, accessible language — and translating them into every dialect imaginable. Everyone deserves to understand humanity's greatest ideas.

When you visit **LibraryofAlexandria.com**, you're not just accessing books — you're joining a global movement to restore, preserve, and share the wisdom of civilization.

Join us today at LibraryofAlexandria.com

Together, we'll ensure the light of human wisdom never fades again.

With gratitude,

The Modern Library of Alexandria Team

Visit:
www.libraryofalexandria.com
Or scan the code below:

Introduction

Thomas Troward and the Foundations of Mental Science

Thomas Troward is one of the most quietly influential figures in the history of modern metaphysical thought. Though less widely known than his successors, such as Napoleon Hill, Joseph Murphy, or even Rhonda Byrne, his teachings form the conceptual foundation upon which much of today's personal development, New Thought, and success literature rests. *The Power of Your Subconscious Mind*—often mistakenly attributed to Murphy but rooted deeply in Troward's philosophy—is not merely a self-help manual; it is a distilled and potent framework for understanding the profound creative intelligence of the human mind.

Born in 1847 in British India and educated in England, Troward served as a divisional judge in the Punjab for many years, steeped in legal reasoning, logic, and philosophical inquiry. It was this rigorous training that informed the unique clarity and precision of his metaphysical ideas. While many spiritual writers of his time drifted into vague mysticism or religious dogma, Troward remained fiercely rational, blending empirical observation with spiritual exploration.

His core thesis is both simple and revolutionary: The mind is the master key of life. Not the surface level of consciousness, but the deeper, more formative realm—the subconscious. This is the domain where our beliefs, assumptions, and mental patterns reside, silently shaping our behavior, outcomes, and destiny. According to Troward, learning to influence this hidden realm is not only possible—it is the very essence of personal power and spiritual evolution.

This book, then, is not about positive thinking in a superficial sense. It is a deep and serious guide to the mechanics of thought, the law of cause and effect in mental action, and the ways in which we can consciously shape our lives from the inside out. Troward's work is not a collection of motivational platitudes, but a philosophical and spiritual treatise—lucid, challenging, and incredibly practical.

Understanding this book requires the reader to appreciate the context in which it was written and the intellectual lineage it belongs to. It is a bridge between 19th-century rationalism and 20th-century spiritual psychology, between the scientific method and mystical experience. It is, in a word, timeless.

The Subconscious: Silent Architect of Your Life

At the heart of this book lies a transformative insight: The subconscious mind is the silent architect of your reality. Whatever is impressed upon it with emotion, repetition, and belief, it will express in form. The subconscious does not reason or question—it accepts whatever the conscious mind repeatedly believes and allows. If the conscious mind is the gardener, the subconscious is the fertile soil. The quality of the crop depends entirely on the seeds sown.

This concept is now echoed in neuroscience, behavioral psychology, and cognitive therapy, but Troward was one of the first to articulate it with such clarity. He explains that most people live as victims of unconscious conditioning—habits, fears, inherited beliefs, and assumptions taken from parents, religion, culture, and past experiences. These internal programs run automatically, manifesting as patterns of success or failure, health or illness, joy or depression.

But Troward does not stop at diagnosis—he offers a prescription. The mind, once understood, can be deliberately directed. Through focused attention, visualization, autosuggestion, and understanding the creative process of thought, the individual can reprogram their subconscious and radically alter their external world. Not through magic, but through the lawful operation of mind.

This is the true meaning of faith in Troward's system—not blind belief, but a scientific certainty that thought is causative. When we consistently hold an idea in mind with conviction, the subconscious accepts it as fact, and the universe begins to organize itself around that internal assumption. This, Troward asserts, is the foundation of all miracles, all healing, all success.

He warns, however, that the subconscious is impartial. It will manifest whatever is impressed upon it—whether positive or negative. This is why worry, fear, resentment, and doubt are so dangerous—not just emotionally, but creatively. They become instructions to the subconscious, and it obeys them without question. Conversely, faith, gratitude, clarity, and expectation are not merely pleasant states—they are active forces of manifestation.

This places enormous responsibility on the individual. You are not a passive recipient of fate, Troward insists. You are a co-creator of reality. Your beliefs shape your biology. Your thoughts become conditions. Your inner speech determines your outer experience. To know this is to reclaim power. To apply it is to become free.

Living Deliberately: From Inner Mastery to Outer Abundance

Troward's ideas are not merely contemplative—they are profoundly actionable. The ultimate purpose of this book is not intellectual understanding, but transformation. It is meant to awaken the reader to a new possibility: That life can be lived deliberately, creatively, and harmoniously, once one masters the inner mechanics of thought.

This mastery begins with awareness. You must become aware of your current thought patterns. Are they serving you? Are they rooted in fear or faith? Are you repeating old assumptions, or consciously choosing new ones? This mental audit is the first step in reclaiming authority over your subconscious.

Next comes discipline. Troward emphasizes the importance of mental concentration—training the mind to dwell on what is wanted, not what is feared. This is not easy. The mind is unruly, prone to distraction and negativity. But with daily practice—through meditation, affirmation, visualization, and mental rehearsal—you begin to change the default programming. You begin to cultivate inner peace, self-confidence, and a felt sense of abundance.

Then comes alignment. Troward believed deeply in the harmony between inner conviction and outer action. Right thinking must be matched by right living. Success, in his view, is not merely the accumulation of wealth or achievement, but the expression of one's highest potential in service to the greater whole. It is the manifestation of one's divine nature in the material world.

This is where his philosophy transcends mere self-help and becomes spiritual. Troward saw every individual as an expression of Infinite Spirit, endowed with the power of creation through thought. To use that power selfishly, ignorantly, or destructively is to suffer. To use it wisely, lovingly, and courageously is to flourish—not just personally, but collectively.

In this sense, *The Power of Your Subconscious Mind* is not just a manual for success—it is a call to higher consciousness. It is an invitation to align your life with divine law, to live from inner truth, and to become a conscious channel through which universal intelligence flows into the world.

That is the essence of power—not domination over others,

but mastery of self. Not control of outcomes, but creative participation in the unfolding of life. Not passive hope, but purposeful imagination.

Read this book not as a consumer, but as a student of the highest science—the science of mind. Study it slowly. Practice it daily. Let it challenge your assumptions and awaken your dormant powers. You are more than flesh and bone, more than a bundle of habits and memories. You are a thinker, a creator, a spiritual being endowed with the power of thought.

And thought, rightly understood and rightly used, is the greatest force in the universe.

Let this book be your guide—not just to success, but to self-realization. Not just to achievement, but to awakening. For once you understand the power of your subconscious mind, you will never again see life the same way. You will see yourself as you truly are—limitless, luminous, and free.

I: The Hidden Power

Chapter 1

To fully understand how much of our everyday life is made up of symbols is to discover the answer to that age-old question: What is Truth? The more we start to recognize this reality, the closer we come to approaching Truth. Understanding Truth means being able to interpret symbols—whether they come from nature or human convention—and translate them into what they actually represent. The source of all human error lies in our failure to do this translation work, and in insisting that symbols have nothing meaningful behind them. Those who have gained this understanding have a great responsibility to help their fellow human beings realize that things have an inner dimension, and that until we know this inner aspect, we don't truly know the things themselves.

Everything has both an inner and outer aspect, and the shallow thinking that prevents us from reaching Truth comes from our tendency to settle for only what we see on the surface. As long as this remains true, it becomes impossible for a person to understand the significance of their own connection to the universe, and this connection is what defines everything we mean by the word "Truth." When someone focuses only on what appears superficial, they cannot make any real progress in gaining knowledge. They are rejecting the principle of "Growth" that forms the foundation of all life—whether spiritual, intellectual, or material—because they fail to consider that everything they observe on the outside can only exist because of some essential principle hidden deep within the core of its existence.

Growth that expands outward from a central point, following a necessary sequence, represents the fundamental Law of Life that governs the entire universe. This principle operates both in the grand unity of cosmic existence and in the individual lives of the smallest organisms. This fundamental concept serves as the key to understanding life's entire mystery, regardless of which level we examine it. Without this essential key, we can never unlock the door that leads from the external appearance of things to their inner reality. Therefore, everyone who has experienced this door opening, even partially, has a responsibility to help others recognize that things possess an inner dimension. Life becomes more authentic and complete as we delve deeper into this inner realm and learn to evaluate everything based on what we can perceive from this interior perspective.

In the broadest sense, everything serves as a symbol of what makes up its inner essence, and all of Nature functions as a gallery of mysteries that reveal profound truths to those who possess the ability to interpret them. However, there exists a more specific sense in which our present life relies on symbols concerning the most significant matters that can engage our minds: the symbols through which we attempt to express the nature and essence of God, and the way in which human life connects to the Divine life. The entire character of a person's life stems from what they genuinely believe about this matter: not their official declaration of faith in a specific doctrine, but what they recognize as the level their mind has truly reached regarding it.

Has someone's mind only reached the point where they believe it's impossible to know anything about God, or to make any practical use of such knowledge if they possessed it? Then their entire inner world exists in a state of confusion, which must inevitably occur when no organizing spirit has yet begun to bring order to the chaos that contains, indeed, the building blocks of existence, but all jumbled and canceling each other out. Has this person taken one step further and recognized that there is a governing and organizing power, but remains ignorant of its true nature beyond this realization? Then the unknown represents something terrifying to them, and surrounded by a storm of fears and anxieties that rob them of all strength to move forward, they spend their life trying to appease this power as something naturally hostile to them, rather than understanding that it is the very heart of their own life and existence.

And so it continues through every level, from the deepest depths of ignorance to the highest peaks of intelligence—a person's life must always perfectly mirror the specific stage they have reached in understanding the divine nature and their own relationship to it. As we move closer to fully grasping Truth, the life-principle within us grows larger, the old restrictions and boundaries that never truly existed begin to fall away from us, and we step into realms of light, freedom, and power that we could never have imagined before. Therefore, it's impossible to overstate how crucial it is to be able to recognize a symbol as just a symbol, and to be able to see through to the inner essence it represents. Life itself can only be understood through the conscious experience of its aliveness within ourselves, and it is our attempt to express these experiences in ways that will spark a similar understanding in others that creates all symbolism.

The closer those we speak to have come to the actual experience, the clearer the symbol becomes; and the farther they are from such experience, the thicker the veil grows; and our entire progress lies in the more and more complete translation of the symbols into increasingly clear statements of what they represent. But the first step, without which all following ones must remain impossible, is to persuade people that symbols are symbols, and not the very Truth itself. And the difficulty lies in this: if the symbolism is adequately effective, it must, to some extent, represent the form of Truth, just as the modeling of drapery suggests the shape of the figure underneath. They possess a certain awareness that somehow they are in the presence of Truth; and this causes people to resist any removal of those folds of drapery which have previously conveyed this idea to their minds.

There are enough signs of inner Truth visible in outward appearances to give fearful people and those who lack the mental strength to think independently an excuse to declare that we've already reached the final answer, and that any additional investigation will only destroy Truth. However, when they make such claims, they reveal their lack of understanding about Truth's fundamental nature—that it cannot be destroyed. The very essence of Truth being Truth makes its destruction impossible. Furthermore, they demonstrate their ignorance of Life's primary principle: the Law of Growth, which continuously drives forward throughout the universe into increasingly vibrant forms of expression, creating expansion everywhere while achieving finality nowhere.

Such uninformed objections don't need to worry us, and we should try to show those who raise them that what they're afraid of is actually the only natural order of Divine Life, which exists "over all, and through all, and in all." However, we must approach this gently, rather than forcefully pushing the source of their fear upon them, which would only drive them away from studying the subject altogether. We should work gradually to help them understand that there's something deeper than what they've previously considered to be ultimate Truth, and help them recognize that the feeling of emptiness and dissatisfaction that occasionally persists in making itself known in their hearts is nothing more than the inner spirit pushing forward to reveal that interior aspect of things which alone can adequately explain what we see on the outside, and without understanding this, we can never truly grasp the real nature of our inheritance in the Universal Life that is Life Everlasting.

Chapter 2

What is this central principle that lies at the foundation of everything? It is Life. However, this isn't life as we understand it through specific forms of expression; it represents something more internal and concentrated than that. It is the "unity of the spirit" which remains unified simply because it hasn't yet transformed into diversity. This concept might be challenging to understand, but it forms the foundation of all scientific understanding of spirit; without it, we lack a shared principle that can explain the countless forms of expression that spirit takes on.

Life represents the complete sum of all its undivided forces, not yet manifesting as any specific form, but containing all possibilities within itself. While this concept is undeniably abstract, it essentially describes the central point from which development occurs through expansion in all directions. This represents the final essence that resists all our attempts at analysis. This truly embodies "the unknowable," not because it cannot be conceived, but because it cannot be broken down into parts. It becomes a matter of perception rather than knowledge, if we define knowledge as the ability that measures relationships between things, since here we have moved beyond any questions of relationships and stand directly before the absolute.

This deepest core of everything is absolute Spirit. It represents Life that hasn't yet been divided into any particular form; it is the universal Life that flows through all things and exists at the center of all manifestations.

To discover this truth is to unlock the secret of power and step into the sacred realm of Living Spirit. Does it seem contradictory to first label this as unknowable, then speak of gaining knowledge of it? It might appear so; however, no less a figure than St. Paul has provided this precedent; for doesn't he describe the ultimate outcome of all explorations into the heights and depths and lengths and breadths of the inner nature of existence as achieving knowledge of that Love which surpasses knowledge. If he can be so boldly contradictory in expression, though not in reality, can't we also speak of understanding "the unknowable"? We can, because this understanding forms the foundation of all other knowledge.

The existence of this undifferentiated universal life-force represents the ultimate foundational truth that all our examination must eventually lead us to discover. No matter what level we conduct our examination on, it must always encounter pure essence, pure energy, pure existence—that which understands itself and acknowledges itself, but which cannot analyze itself because it isn't constructed from separate components, but is fundamentally complete: it is absolute Unity. However, examination that doesn't result in synthesis is simply destructive: it resembles a child carelessly tearing apart a flower and discarding the pieces, rather than a botanist who also dismantles the flower but constructs in his mind from those carefully examined pieces a comprehensive synthesis of Nature's creative force, encompassing the principles governing the formation of all flower varieties. The worth of examination lies in guiding us to the original source of whatever we study, and thereby teaching us the principles through which its ultimate form emerges from this center.

Understanding how something is constructed, we transform our analysis into synthesis, and in doing so we develop a capacity for creation that will always remain beyond the grasp of those who consider "the unknowable" to be the same as "non-existence."

This concept of the unknowable forms the foundation of all materialism; yet no scientist, regardless of how materialistic their tendencies may be, approaches this unanalyzable remainder in such a manner when encountering it in their laboratory experiments. Instead, they make this final unanalyzable fact the foundation of their synthesis. They discover that ultimately it represents energy of some form, whether expressed as heat or motion; however, they do not abandon their scientific endeavors simply because they cannot analyze it any further. They take exactly the opposite approach, recognizing that the conservation of energy, its indestructible nature, and the impossibility of increasing or decreasing the total amount of energy in the world, constitutes the one solid and unchanging fact upon which the entire structure of physical science must be constructed. They ground all their knowledge upon their understanding of "the unknowable." This approach is correct, because if they could break down this energy into additional components, then the same challenge of "the unknowable" would still confront them. All our advancement involves continuously pushing the unknowable, in terms of the unanalyzable remainder, one step further back; but the notion that there should be no ultimate unanalyzable remainder anywhere represents an unthinkable concept.

In recognizing the undifferentiated unity of Living Spirit as the central fact of any system, whether we're looking at the system of the entire universe or a single organism, we are following a strictly scientific method. We continue our analysis until it inevitably leads us to this final fact, and then we accept this fact as the foundation of our synthesis. The Science of Spirit is therefore no less scientific than the Science of Matter; furthermore, it begins from the same initial fact, the fact of a living energy that resists definition or explanation, wherever we encounter it; but it differs from the science of matter in that it views this energy through the lens of responsive intelligence which doesn't fall within the scope of physical science as such. The Science of Spirit and the Science of Matter are not in opposition. They complement each other, and neither can be fully understood without some knowledge of the other; and, being essentially two parts of one whole, they gradually blend into each other in a borderland where no arbitrary line can be drawn between them. Science studied in a genuinely scientific spirit, pursuing its own deductions fearlessly to their logical conclusions, will always reveal the dual nature of things, the inner and the outer; and it is only an incomplete and damaged science that refuses to acknowledge both.

Studying the material world doesn't necessarily lead to Materialism, provided we allow this study to reach its natural conclusion. Materialism represents a narrow perspective of the universe that refuses to acknowledge anything beyond the mechanical effects of mechanical causes. Any system that recognizes no higher power than the physical forces of nature must logically end up with no higher final recourse than physical force, or alternatively, deception. I'm referring, naturally, to the inherent tendency of such a system, not to the moral character of individuals, who often demonstrate much higher standards than the systems they claim to follow. However, since we want to prevent the spread of a way of thinking whose consequences history has demonstrated all too clearly—whether in Borgia-era Italy, Revolutionary France, or during the Commune of the Franco-Prussian War—we should dedicate ourselves to examining the inner and spiritual dimension of existence. This dimension forms the foundation of a system whose logical outcomes are truth and love rather than betrayal and violence.

Some of us have undoubtedly wondered why the Heavenly Jerusalem is described in the Book of Revelation as a cube; "the length and the breadth and the height of it are equal." This is because the cube represents perfect stability, and therefore symbolizes Truth, which can never be overthrown. No matter which side you turn it to, it remains the perfect cube, always standing upright; it cannot be toppled. This shape, therefore, represents the physical manifestation in solid form of that central life-giving energy, which is not itself confined to any single plane but creates all planes—the planes above and below and on all four sides. Yet it is simultaneously a city, a place where people live; and this is because what exists "within" is Living Spirit, which makes its home there.

Just as one face of a cube suggests all the other faces and the interior space within, any level of physical reality suggests the others and the inner source that creates them all. If we want to make real progress in understanding the spiritual dimension of science—and every field of science has a spiritual dimension—we must always keep our attention focused on this "deepest inner core" that holds the potential for all outward expression, the "fourth dimension" that creates the cube. Our everyday language shows how naturally we recognize this truth. We talk about the spirit behind an action, getting into the spirit of a game, the spirit of an era, and similar expressions. In every case, our intuition recognizes spirit as the true essence of things. We only lose our genuine understanding of their nature when we start analyzing them from the outside rather than from the inside.

The scientific study of spirit involves intelligently pursuing and systematically following the same principle that currently only appears to us occasionally in fleeting and unclear glimpses. Once we understand that this universal and boundless power of spirit forms the foundation of all things and of ourselves as well, we have discovered the key to the entire situation; and no matter how extensively we advance our studies in spiritual science, we will find nothing but specific expressions of this one universal principle. "The Kingdom of Heaven is within you."

Chapter 3

I have emphasized that the "innermost core" of all things is living Spirit, and that the Science of Spirit differs from the Science of Matter because it examines Energy through the lens of responsive intelligence, which falls outside the realm of physical science as we know it. These are the two essential concepts we must grasp if we want to maintain a clear understanding of Spiritual Science and avoid being confused by arguments that come only from the physical side of Science—the living nature of the originating principle that exists at the center of all things, and its intelligent and responsive character. Its living quality is evident to our observation, at least from the point where we recognize it in the plant kingdom; but its intelligence and responsiveness may not be immediately apparent. However, a little reflection will quickly lead us to recognize this aspect as well.

No one can deny that there's an intelligent order throughout all of nature, since it takes the highest intelligence of our most highly-trained minds to follow the steps of this universal intelligence that's always ahead of them. The more deeply we investigate the world we live in, the clearer it must become to us that all our science is simply the translation into words or numerical symbols of that order which already exists. If clearly stating this existing order is the highest achievement the human intellect can reach, this surely suggests a corresponding intelligence in the power that gives rise to this great sequence of order and interrelation, creating one harmonious whole. Now, unless we fall back on the idea of a craftsman working on material outside of himself—in which case we'd have to explain the phenomenon of the craftsman—the only way we can understand this power is that it's the Living Spirit inherent in the heart of every atom, giving it outward form and definition, and becoming within it those intrinsic polarities that make up its characteristic nature.

There is no random work here. Every attraction and repulsion operates with its appropriate force, gathering atoms into molecules, molecules into tissues, tissues into organs, and organs into individuals. At each stage of this progression, we obtain the sum of the intelligent forces that work within the component parts, plus a higher level of intelligence that we can consider as the collective intelligence superior to that of the simple sum-total of the parts, something that belongs to the individual as a complete entity, and not to the parts themselves. These are facts that can be thoroughly demonstrated through physical science; and they also provide a fundamental law in spiritual science, which is that in any collective body the intelligence of the whole surpasses that of the sum of the parts.

Spirit lies at the foundation of everything, and careful observation reveals that its workings are directed by perfect intelligence that matches methods to goals and brings harmony to the entire universe of visible existence in those remarkable ways that physical science makes clearer with each passing day; and this intelligence must exist within the creating spirit itself, since there is no other place from which it could come. Based on these reasons, therefore, we can clearly state that Spirit is intelligent, and that everything it accomplishes is achieved through the intelligent matching of methods to goals.

But Spirit also responds to influence. Here we must return to the principle mentioned earlier: the combined intelligence of Spirit expressed through lower forms of manifestation cannot match the intelligence of the complete whole when considered as a unified entity. This fundamental principle cannot be emphasized strongly enough in our understanding. The level of spiritual intelligence corresponds directly to the completeness of the organism through which it expresses itself. Therefore, a more highly developed being possesses a degree of spirit that surpasses and can consequently control all lower or less completely integrated levels of spirit. Understanding this relationship helps us begin to comprehend why the spirit that exists as the "innermost essence within" all things demonstrates both intelligence and responsiveness.

Being intelligent, spirit knows, and since spirit is ultimately all that exists, what it knows is itself. Therefore, it is the power that recognizes itself; consequently, its lower powers recognize its higher powers, and through the law of attraction, they are compelled to respond to the higher aspects of themselves. Based on this general principle, spirit, regardless of whatever external form it takes, is necessarily intelligent and responsive. However, intelligence and responsiveness suggest personality; and we may therefore now take a step further and argue that all spirit contains the elements of personality, even though, in any specific case, it may not yet be expressed as that individual personality which we find in ourselves.

In essence, spirit is inherently personal by nature, even when it hasn't yet reached the level of integration necessary to express itself as personal in its outward form. Within us, this integration has advanced sufficiently to achieve that level, which is why we recognize ourselves as expressions of personality. The human realm represents the domain where this personality manifests—a personality that forms the core of spiritual essence across all dimensions of existence. To express this entire concept more simply, we can say that our individual personality must have originated from something that is itself personal, based on the principle that you cannot extract more from a container than what it actually holds.

In ourselves, we discover a more complete integration of spirit into physical form that is missing in the lower levels of nature. Since spirit naturally knows itself and must recognize its own levels in different forms, the spirit in all stages below human personality is compelled to respond to itself in that higher level that makes up human individuality. This forms the foundation of human thought's ability to express itself outwardly in countless forms of its own creation.

But if the subordination of the lower levels of consciousness to the higher ones is one of the fundamental laws that underlies the creative power of thought, there is another equally fundamental law that places a beneficial restraint on the misuse of that power. It is the law that we can control the forces of the universe for our own purposes only to the extent that we first understand and follow their basic nature. We can use water for any purpose that doesn't require it to flow uphill, and we can harness electricity for any purpose that doesn't require it to move from a lower to a higher potential.

So it is with that universal power we call the Spirit. It possesses an inherent general nature that we must work with if we want to use it for our specific goals, and this nature can be summarized in one word: "goodness." The Spirit is Life, so its general tendency must always be toward life or toward increasing the vitality of every individual. And because it is universal, it cannot have particular interests to serve, so its action must always be equally beneficial to everyone. This is the general nature of spirit; and just as water, electricity, or any other physical force in the universe will not work against its general nature, Spirit will not work against its general nature.

The conclusion is clear. If we want to use Spirit, we must follow the law of the Spirit, which is "Goodness." This is the only restriction. If our original intention is good, we can use the spiritual power for whatever purpose we choose. And how should "goodness" be defined? Simply by the child's understanding that what is bad is not good, and that what is good is not bad; we all know the difference between bad and good instinctively. If we conform to this principle of obedience to the fundamental law of the Spirit, all that remains is for us to study the law of proportion that exists between the more and less fully integrated forms of Spirit, and then apply our knowledge with determination.

Chapter 4

The spiritual law that our investigation has brought us to encompasses an incredibly broad range. We've traced it from the concept of spiritual intelligence existing in the fundamental atoms all the way to the gathering of this intelligence as the conscious identity of each person. However, there's no reason this law should stop working at this stage, or at any stage before reaching the complete whole. The measure of whether any principle is valid lies in its ability to function just as effectively on a grand scale as it does on a small one—while the character of its domain is shaped by the principle's own nature, the reach of that domain knows no bounds. Therefore, if we keep following this law we've been examining, it brings us to the idea of an intelligence unit that surpasses individual human intelligence by the same degree that a person's unified intelligence exceeds the intelligence of any single atom in their body. In this way, we can imagine a collective individuality that embodies the spiritual nature of any group of people—whether they're residents of a city, a region, a nation, or the entire globe.

The process doesn't have to end there. Following this same principle, there would be a higher collective individuality for all of humanity throughout the entire solar system, and ultimately we arrive at the idea of a supreme intelligence that brings together within itself the collective individualities of every system in the universe. This isn't just a wild fantasy. We discover this as the law that forms our own conscious individuality, and we see the same principle operating everywhere on the physical level. Physical science recognizes this as the "law of inverse squares," where the forces of mutual attraction or repulsion aren't simply equal to the sum of forces produced by the two bodies involved, but equal to these two forces multiplied together and divided by the square of the distance separating them, creating a resulting power that continuously increases at a rapidly accelerating rate as the two mutually influencing bodies move closer to each other.

Since this law applies universally throughout the physical world, the principle of continuity provides strong reason to believe that a similar pattern exists in the spiritual realm. We should always keep in mind the ancient wisdom that "a truth on one level is a truth on all levels." If a principle exists at all, it exists everywhere. We must not let ourselves be fooled by surface appearances; we need to remember that the visible outcomes of any principle's operation involve two elements—the principle itself, which is the active component, and the material it works upon, which is the passive component; and while the first element remains constant, the second varies, meaning that when the same unchanging force acts upon different variables, it must naturally create different results. This becomes clear immediately when we express it in mathematical terms; for instance, a, b or c, when multiplied by x, produce the results ax, bx, cx respectively, which differ significantly from each other, even though the factor x stays exactly the same.

This principle of generating power through attraction operates in the spiritual realm just as it does in the physical world, functioning with identical mathematical accuracy in both domains. Therefore, human individuality doesn't simply consist of a collection of its components, whether spiritual or physical, but rather emerges from the unified power that results when these components form intimate connections with one another. This unity, following the law of power generation through attraction, possesses vastly greater intelligence and strength than any less completely integrated form of consciousness. In this way, a natural principle that governs both physical and spiritual laws completely explains every claim that has ever been made about our thoughts' creative power over everything that enters the sphere of our personal existence. This is why each person stands at the center of their own universe and possesses the ability to control everything within it by directing their thoughts.

However, as I mentioned earlier, there's no reason this principle shouldn't be understood as expanding outward from the individual person until it encompasses the entire universe. Every person, standing at the center of their own world, is simultaneously positioned within a larger system where they represent just one of countless similar elements, and this system exists within an even greater one, continuing upward until we arrive at the ultimate center of everything; wisdom and strength grow from one center to the next at a rate that increases with unimaginable speed, following the law we are currently examining, until they reach their peak in unlimited wisdom and strength that matches the scope of All-Being.

Now we have seen that man's relationship to the lower forms of spirit is one of superiority and command, but what is his relationship to these higher forms? In any harmoniously structured system, the relationship of the part to the whole never interferes with the free operation of the part in performing its own functions; on the contrary, it is precisely through this relationship that each part is maintained in a position to carry out all functions for which it is suited. Therefore, the subordination of the individual person to the supreme mind, far from limiting his freedom, is the very condition that makes freedom possible, or even life itself. The general movement of the whole necessarily carries the part along with it; and as long as the part allows itself to be carried forward in this way, there will be no obstacle to its free functioning in any direction for which it is suited by its own individuality. This truth was expressed in the ancient Hindu religion as the Car of Jaggarnath—an ideal car only, which later generations degraded into a terribly material symbol. "Jaggarnath" means "Lord of the Universe," and thus represents the Universal Mind. This, by the law of Being, must always move forward regardless of any attempts by individuals to restrain it. Those who climb upon its car move onward with it toward endlessly advancing evolution, while those who seek to oppose it must be crushed beneath its wheels, for it shows no favoritism to anyone.

If we want to use the universal law of spirit to control our own small individual worlds, we must also recognize it in relation to the supreme center around which we ourselves revolve. But not in the old way of assuming that this center is a whimsical Individual outside of ourselves, who can be appeased or persuaded into giving the good that he is not good enough to give on his own initiative. As long as we hold onto this childish idea, we have not entered into the freedom that comes from knowing the certainty of Law. Supreme Mind is Supreme Law, and can be counted on with the same precision as when it appears in any of the specific laws of the physical world; and the result of studying, understanding and following this Supreme Law is that we gain the power to use it. We don't need to fear it with the old fear that comes from ignorance, because we can confidently rely on the principle that the whole cannot have any interest that goes against the parts that make it up; and likewise, the part cannot have any interest that goes against the whole.

Our lack of understanding about how we relate to the greater whole might make it seem like we have separate interests, but deeper knowledge will always reveal this idea to be false. Because of this, the same spiritual responsiveness that shows up as obedience to our desires when we focus on those levels of spirit that are below our own individual nature must show up as an essential flow of wisdom and strength when we turn our attention to the infinite spirit, of which our individual self is a unique expression, since when we look upward in this way we are seeking the higher aspects of ourselves.

The increased vitality of the parts means the increased vitality of the whole, and since it is impossible to think of spirit in any other way than as a continuously expanding principle of Life, the need for such increased vitality must, by the inherent nature of spirit, be fulfilled by a corresponding supply of continually growing intelligence and power. Therefore, by a natural law, the need creates the supply, and this supply may be freely applied to any and every subject matter that appeals to us. There is no limit to the supply of this energy other than what we ourselves impose upon it through our thought; nor is there any limit to the purposes we may make it serve other than the one grand Law of Order, which states that good things used for wrong purposes become evil. The consideration of the intelligent and responsive nature of spirit reveals that there can be no limitations but these. The first is a limitation inherent in spirit itself, and the second is a limitation which has no foundation except in our own ignorance.

It's true that to keep our healthy actions within our own personal world, we must constantly move forward alongside the larger whole that we're part of. However, this doesn't mean there's any limit on our freedom to make the most of our lives according to those universal principles of life that form our foundation. There isn't one law for the individual part and a different law for the whole—the same law of Being flows through both equally. Therefore, as we come to understand the true law of our own individuality, we'll discover that it aligns with the law of progress for the human race. The collective individuality of humanity is simply the personal individuality reproduced on a grander scale. Any action that genuinely develops the inherent powers of the individual must naturally align with that forward movement of the universal mind, which represents the evolution of humanity as a whole.

Selfishness represents a limited understanding of who we truly are, causing us to lose sight of our position within the greater whole and failing to recognize that our very life springs from this connection. It reflects ignorance about our true potential and results in restricting our own capabilities. Therefore, if the clear evidence of harmonious relationships throughout the physical world inevitably points to an intelligent spirit as the deepest essence within all things, we must also acknowledge ourselves as individual expressions of this same spirit that manifests throughout the universe as the force of intelligent responsiveness known as Love.

We discover that we are an essential and integral part of the Infinite Harmony of All-Being; not simply recognizing this profound truth as a vague intuition, but as the logical and inevitable outcome of the universal Life-principle that flows through all of Nature. We realize our intuition was correct because we have uncovered the law that created it; and now intuition and investigation both come together in revealing our own individual position in the grand design of existence. Even the most enlightened among us have, so far, little more than the faintest glimpse of what this position truly is. It is the position of power. In relation to those higher forms of spirit that we call "the universal," the law of humanity's deepest nature makes each person like a lens, drawing into the focus of their own individuality all that they desire of light and power in streams of endless abundance; and toward the lower forms of spirit, which create for each person the realm of their own particular world, humanity thus becomes the guiding center of energy and order.

Can we imagine any situation that holds greater potential than this? The sphere of this life-giving influence can grow larger as a person develops a broader understanding of their connection with Infinite Being; however, it would be impossible to create a more complete law governing this relationship. Emerson correctly observed that a small amount of algebra will often accomplish much more in clarifying our thoughts than extensive poetic comparisons. From an algebraic perspective, it becomes obvious that any difference between various powers of x vanishes when compared to x multiplied by itself infinitely, since no relationship can exist between any finite power, no matter how large, and infinity; therefore, the connection between the individual and All-Being must always stay constant.

But this doesn't interfere with the law of growth, through which individuals rise to increasingly higher levels of their own individuality. The unchanging relationship between all specific powers of x and infinity doesn't affect how the different powers of x relate to each other; instead, the fact that we can mentally conceive of multiplying x by itself infinitely is actually proof that there's no limit to how far we can raise x in its specific powers.

I trust that readers without a mathematical background will forgive me for using this approach to present the information for the benefit of others who will find it convincing. Once a relationship is clearly understood from a mathematical perspective, it becomes one of the unchanging truths of the universe from that point forward—no longer something to debate, but a fundamental principle that can be accepted as the foundation upon which to construct the structure of additional knowledge. However, setting aside mathematical formulas, we can say that because the Infinite is infinite, there can be no boundary to how extensively the vital principle of growth may draw from it, and therefore there is no boundary to the expansion of an individual's abilities. Because we are what we are, we may become what we choose to be.

The Kabbalists speak of "the lost word," a word of power that humanity has misplaced. For anyone who finds this word, all things become possible. Has this miraculous word truly been lost? Both yes and no. It represents the open secret of the universe, and the Bible provides us with the key to understanding it. Scripture tells us, "The Word is near you, even in your mouth and in your heart." This is the most familiar word of all, the word that we recognize in our hearts as the center of our conscious existence, and which passes through our lips a hundred times each day. This word is "I AM." Because I am what I am, I can become what I choose to be. My individuality serves as one of the ways through which the Infinite expresses itself, and therefore I am myself that very power which I discover to be the deepest essence within all things.

To me, understanding the great unity of all Spirit, the infinite is not something vague or undefined, because I see it as the infinite of Myself. It is the very same I AM that I am; and this happens not through any uncertain act of favor, but through the law of polarity which forms the foundation of all Nature. The law of polarity is the principle by which everything reaches completion by expressing itself in the opposite direction from where it began. It is the simple law that shows there can be no inside without an outside, nor one end of a stick without the other end.

Life is movement, and all movement represents energy appearing at a different location and, whenever work has been accomplished, in a different form from its original state; however, wherever this energy emerges again and in whatever new shape it takes, the life-giving force remains unchanged. This is simply the scientific principle of energy conservation, and our understanding of ourselves as essential parts of the vast universal power rests on this well-established concept.

We would be wise to listen carefully to the words of great teachers who have shown us that all power exists within the "I AM," and to embrace this teaching through faith in their simple authority rather than reject it entirely; however, the better path is to understand why they taught this way, and to discover for ourselves this fundamental law that all master minds have understood throughout history. It is truly accurate that the "lost word" is the one we know best, always present in our hearts and spoken by our lips. We have not lost the word itself, but rather our understanding of its power. And as the endless layers of meaning that the words I AM contain begin to reveal themselves to us, we start to grasp the incredible truth that we ourselves are the very power we have been searching for.

It is the focusing of Spirit from the universal into the individual, bringing with it all its inherent powers, just as the smallest flame contains all the qualities of fire. The I AM in the individual is the same as the I AM in the universal. It is the same Power operating in the smaller sphere where the individual serves as the center. This is the great truth that the ancients expressed through the concept of the Macrocosm and the Microcosm, where the lesser I

AM reflects the exact image of the greater, and which the Bible describes when it speaks of man as the image of God.

The tremendous practical significance of this principle lies in how it provides the key to understanding the fundamental law that "as a person thinks, so they become." People frequently ask why this happens, and the explanation can be presented this way: We understand through our own experience that we recognize our aliveness in two distinct ways—through our ability to take action and our capacity to experience feelings. When we think about Spirit in its absolute form, we can only imagine it as these same two expressions of life extended to infinity. This means infinite responsiveness. There cannot be any doubt about the level of sensitivity involved, because Spirit itself is pure sensitivity, making it infinitely moldable to even the slightest influence applied to it. Therefore, every thought we create sends out its vibrating energy into the infinite realm of Spirit, generating currents there that share the same characteristics but possess far greater strength.

Spirit in the Infinite represents the Creative Power of the universe, and when our thoughts interact with it, they set a genuine creative force into motion. If this principle applies to one thought, it applies to all thoughts, which means we are constantly creating a world around ourselves that precisely reflects the nature of our own thinking. Thoughts that persist naturally create a stronger external impact than random ones that lack focus on any specific goal. Scattered thoughts that don't recognize any unifying principle will fail to manifest any unifying principle. The thought that we are powerless and cannot influence our circumstances leads to an inability to control those circumstances, while thoughts of power generate actual power.

At every moment, we're working with an incredibly sensitive medium that awakens creative forces, giving shape to even our smallest thought vibrations. This power exists within us because of our spiritual essence, and we can't separate ourselves from it. It represents our truly amazing inheritance because it's a force that, if not wisely directed into organized activity, will release its uncontrolled energy in destructive ways. If it isn't used for building up, it will tear down. And there's nothing unusual about this: it's simply the same principle appearing again on the universal and undifferentiated level that runs through all of Nature's forces. Which of these forces isn't destructive unless channeled into some specific direction? Steam that builds up, electricity that accumulates, water that gathers will eventually burst forth, bringing destruction everywhere; but when directed through proper channels, they become sources of constructive power, as limitless as Nature itself.

And here let me pause to draw attention to this concept of accumulation. The greater the buildup of energy, the greater the danger if it isn't channeled into proper order, and the greater the power if it is. Fortunately for humanity, physical forces like electricity don't usually exist in highly concentrated forms. Occasionally circumstances combine to create such concentration, but typically the elements of power are distributed more or less evenly. In the same way, for most of humanity, this spiritual power hasn't yet reached a very high level of concentration. Every mind, it's true, must be somewhat of a center of concentration, because otherwise it would have no conscious individuality; but the power of the individualized mind rapidly increases as it recognizes its unity with the Infinite life, and its thought-currents, whether well or poorly directed, then take on proportionately great significance.

Therefore, the harmful effects of misdirected thinking are somewhat reduced among most people, and various influences work to guide their thoughts in the right direction, even though these thinkers don't understand what the power of thought actually is. Much religious teaching aims to properly direct the thoughts of those who lack understanding, and these uninformed individuals must accept such guidance through faith in simple authority because they cannot grasp its true meaning. However, despite these forms of assistance available to humanity, the overall flow of uncontrolled thinking inevitably tends toward negative outcomes, which is why the educated mind focuses its energy on breaking free from the tangles of chaotic thought and helping others achieve the same freedom. Breaking free from this entanglement means reaching complete Liberty, which equals complete Power.

Chapter 6

The confusion we must break free from stems from the exact same principle that creates freedom and strength. It's the identical principle working under reversed circumstances. I want to emphasize a crucial law: any process carried out in reverse order will inevitably produce the opposite outcome. This concept explains a great deal about life's challenges. The physical world provides countless examples of how "inversion" operates. In a dynamo, the process begins with mechanical force that eventually transforms into the more refined power of electricity. However, reverse this sequence by starting with electricity generation, and it converts into mechanical force, as we see in motors. In one direction, a spinning wheel creates electricity, while in the reverse direction, electricity creates a spinning wheel. To demonstrate this same principle using basic mathematics: if $10 \div 2 = 5$, then $10 \div 5 = 2$. "Inversion" represents an enormously important factor that must be considered. However, I can only outline the general principle here: the same force can create completely opposite effects when applied under opposite conditions. Medieval "magicians" expressed this truth through two triangles positioned inversely to each other. We often make the error of assuming that opposite results require opposite forces to create them. Our understanding of things becomes much clearer when we realize this isn't true—

the same force will generate opposite results depending on which pole it originates from.

Therefore, the reverse use of the same principle that creates freedom and power forms the trap we must escape before we can achieve power and freedom, and this principle is captured in the law that "as a man thinks so he is." This represents the fundamental law of the human mind. It is Descartes' "cogito, ergo sum." When we track consciousness back to its source, we discover that it is entirely subjective. Our external senses would stop functioning if not for the subjective consciousness that perceives what they relay to it.

The concept that reaches our conscious awareness might be incorrect, but until a more accurate idea forcefully replaces it, that concept remains a real and substantial truth for the mind that brings it into being. I once witnessed a man talking to a tree stump that appeared like a person standing in a garden under the moonlight, repeatedly asking for its name and what it wanted; from the speaker's perspective, the garden truly contained a living person who simply wouldn't respond. In this way, every mind exists in a reality shaped by its own perceptions. These perceptions might be mistaken, but they still form the actual reality of existence for the mind that creates them. We cannot live any life other than the one we experience within our own minds; therefore, the progress of humanity as a whole relies on replacing ideas of evil, oppression, and chaos with concepts of good, liberty, and order. This transformation can only happen by providing compelling reasons to embrace new ideas instead of old ones. For every individual, our beliefs become our reality, and these beliefs can only change when we find solid grounds for adopting different beliefs.

This briefly explains the reasoning behind the principle that "as a man thinks so he is," and all of life's outcomes flow from how this principle operates. When a person first understands the law of cause and effect as it relates to their own behavior, they realize that results always reflect the nature of their causes. Since their reasoning comes only from observing the external world, they see external actions as the only causes they can truly control. Therefore, when they develop enough moral awareness to recognize that many of their actions have deserved consequences, they begin to fear punishment as the natural outcome. Then, because of the law that "thoughts are things," the troubles they fear take shape and throw them into difficult situations, which in turn lead them to commit more wrong actions. These generate new fears that also become real problems, creating a cycle from which there is no escape as long as the person believes that only their external actions have the power to influence their surrounding world.

This is the Law of Works, the Circle of Karma, the Wheel of Fate, from which there seems to be no way out, because completely fulfilling the law of our moral nature today is only enough for today and leaves nothing extra to make up for yesterday's failures. This is the inevitable law of things as they appear when we only observe them from the outside; and as long as this understanding persists, the law of each person's inner consciousness makes it real for them. What we need, therefore, is to establish the understanding that external actions are NOT the only force that creates effects, but that there is another law of cause and effect, specifically, that of pure Thought. This is the Law of Faith, the Law of Liberty; because it introduces us to a power that can start a new chain of cause and effect that is not connected to any past actions.

But this shift in mindset can't happen until we grasp some truth that gives us a solid reason to change. We need firm ground to stand on when we believe in this higher principle. In the end, we discover this foundation in the great Truth about the eternal connection between universal spirit and individual spirit. When we understand that essentially nothing exists except spirit, and that we ourselves are individual expressions of the Intelligence and Love that govern the universe, we reach solid ground where we discover we can direct our Thought to create whatever effect we choose. We move beyond the concept of two opposing forces that need to be reconciled, and into understanding a duality where the only opposition is between the inner and outer aspects of the same unity—the polarity that exists naturally in all Being. We then realize that because of this unity, our Thought possesses unlimited creative power, and it's free to go wherever it chooses, and isn't bound to accept as unavoidable the consequences that would result from our past actions if left unchecked by renewed thinking.

In its own independent creative power, the mind has discovered the way out of the deadly cycle in which its earlier ignorance of the highest law had trapped it. The Unity of the Spirit is discovered to result in complete Liberty; the old sequence of Karma has been severed, and a new and higher order has been established. In the old order, the line of thought received its character from the character of the actions, and since they always fell short of perfection, the development of a higher thought-power from this source was impossible. This is the order in which everything is viewed from the outside. It is a reversed order. But in the true order, everything is viewed from the inside.

It is our thoughts that determine the quality of our actions, not the other way around, and since thought is free, it has the liberty to focus on the highest principles, which then naturally express themselves in our outward behavior, so that both our thoughts and actions align with the great eternal laws and become unified in purpose with the Universal Mind. A person realizes that they are no longer bound by the consequences of their past actions, performed during their time of ignorance, and in fact, that they were never truly bound by them except to the extent that they gave these consequences power through false understanding of the truth; and by recognizing themselves for what they truly are—the expression of the Infinite Spirit in individual form—they discover that they are free, that they are a "partaker of Divine nature," not losing their identity, but becoming more and more fully themselves with ever-expanding perfection, following a path of evolution whose possibilities are limitless.

However, not everyone possesses this understanding. Most people continue to view God as a separate Being existing outside themselves, and what the more enlightened person recognizes as unity of consciousness and shared essence appears to the less developed as an external peace treaty between conflicting personalities. This gives rise to the entire spectrum of concepts that can be called the Messianic Idea. This idea is not, as some appear to believe, a misunderstanding of the truth of existence. Instead, when properly comprehended, it reveals the most expansive understanding of that truth; and only from the foundation of this highest knowledge could such a comprehensive idea, perfectly suited to every type of mind, have been developed. It represents the transformation of relationships emerging from the most fundamental laws of existence into language that even the most uneducated can grasp; a transformation crafted with such masterful expertise that, as consciousness develops spiritually, each level of progress encounters a matching revelation of Divine significance; while even the most basic understanding of the underlying concept provides sufficient foundation for a complete transformation of one's thoughts about oneself, establishing a firm position from which to view oneself as no longer constrained by the law of punishment for previous wrongdoings, but as liberated to pursue the new principle of Freedom as a child of God.

The person's understanding of how this liberation works might involve the most crude human-like descriptions of God or the most simplistic ideas about satisfying Divine justice through someone else taking their place, but the practical outcome remains identical. They have found something that gives them a satisfactory basis for viewing themselves in a completely new way; and since the conditions of our inner consciousness form the actual realities of our existence, providing them with a persuasive reason for believing themselves to be free is the same as making them free.

As he gains more understanding, he may discover that his initial explanation of how things work was insufficient; but when he reaches this point, further study will reveal that the great truth of his freedom stands on a more solid foundation than the traditional interpretation of established beliefs, and that it has its origins in the fundamental laws of Nature, which are never uncertain, and which can never be overthrown. And it is exactly because their entire operation has its foundation in the unchanging laws of Mind that there exists a constant need for offering to people something they can grasp as an adequate basis for that shift in mental perspective, through which alone they can be saved from the destructive cycle that is represented by the symbol of the Old Serpent.

The hope and glimpse of such a new principle has formed the core of all religions throughout history, no matter how poorly understood by uninformed believers; and, regardless of what our personal views might be concerning the historical facts of Christianity, we will discover that the great figure of liberated and perfected humanity at its center satisfies this longing of all peoples by presenting their grand ideal of Divine power stepping in to save humanity by becoming united with it. This is the concept presented to us, whether we understand it in the most literally physical sense, or as the ideal representation of the deepest philosophical examination of mental laws, or in whatever combination of ways we might blend these two extremes. The fundamental idea impressed upon the mind must always remain the same: it is that there exists a Divine authorization for knowing ourselves to be the children of God and "partakers of the Divine nature"; and when we recognize in this way that there is solid foundation for believing ourselves free, through the very force of this belief we become free.

The right result of studying the spiritual laws that form the inner nature of all things is not to satisfy mere idle curiosity or to gain supernatural abilities, but to achieve our spiritual freedom, without which no further growth is possible. Once we reach this destination, the old things have disappeared and everything has become new. The mystical seven days of the original creation have been completed, and the first day of the new week begins for us with its resurrection to a new life, expressing on the highest level that great teaching of the "octave" which the knowledge of the ancient temples traced throughout Nature, and which today's science confirms, though unaware of its ultimate meaning.

When we achieve this freedom by recognizing our unity with Infinite Being, we reach the end of the old chain of events and discover the beginning point of something new. The former restrictions we experienced never actually existed except in our own misunderstanding of reality, and they disappear one after another as we move forward into greater clarity. We discover that the Life-Spirit we have been searching for exists within us; and with this as our foundation, our connection to everything else becomes part of an amazing living Order where each component works in harmony with the whole, and the whole works in harmony with each component, creating a symphony as vast as infinity itself, where the only boundaries are those established by the Law of Love.

I have tried in this short series of articles to outline briefly the main points of connection between Spirit within ourselves and in our environment. This topic has occupied human thinking from ancient times to today, and no single thinker can ever expect to understand it completely. However, there are certain basic principles that we must all understand, no matter how we might focus our detailed studies, and I have attempted to point these out, with whatever level of success the reader must decide for themselves. Let the reader, though, hold firmly to this one essential truth, and the development of additional truth from it becomes simply a matter of time—that there is only One Spirit, regardless of how many forms its expressions may take, and that "the Unity of the Spirit is the Bond of Peace."

II: The Perversion Of Truth

There is a very general recognition, which is growing day by day more and more widespread, that there is a kind of hidden power somewhere that we have the ability to use somehow. The ideas on this subject are extremely vague for most people, but they are still taking on a more and more definite form, and what they appear to be becoming for the general public is the recognition of the power of suggestion. I suppose none of us doubts that there is such a thing as the power of suggestion and that it can produce very great results indeed, and that it is above all a hidden power; it works behind the scenes, it works through what we know as the subconscious mind, and consequently its activity is not immediately recognizable, nor is the source from which it comes. Now there is, in some aspects, its usefulness, its benefit, but in other aspects there is a source of danger, because a power of this kind is obviously one that can be used either well or poorly; in itself it is perfectly neutral, it all depends on the purpose for which it is used, and the character of the person who employs it.

This awareness of suggestion's power is often taking a very troubling direction, and I draw your attention to countless advertisements in certain types of magazines—many of you have surely encountered numerous examples of this sort—that promise, for a specific amount of money, to teach you how to gain personal influence, mental power, and the power of suggestion, as these advertisements quite brazenly claim, for whatever purpose you might want. Some even provide more specific details, explaining the exact kinds of purposes for which you can use this power, all of which are certainly uses that no one should ever attempt to make of it.

Therefore, this understanding of suggestion's power, even when viewed simply as a way to make money, not to mention other misuses of it, is becoming popular among certain groups of people who don't see the higher potential in these matters. It's unfortunate that this happens, but it's naturally unavoidable. You have a power that can be used positively, and that can be used negatively, that can be used for noble purposes, and can be used for base purposes, and as a result you will find many people who, as soon as they discover it, will immediately think only of the lower purposes, not the higher ones.

To support what I'm saying—though this certainly isn't meant as a trivial example, and is probably intended as something more significant, but I can't say I agree with it—I want to show you that I'm speaking from real facts by reading you a note I've taken from the Daily Mail of January 20th, which I'm sure some of you may have seen. The article is titled "Killing by Prayer," and it describes how a particular circular has been distributed to various hospitals and other institutions where vivisection research takes place. In this circular, signed with the initials "M. C.," the author explains that they accidentally learned about someone who regularly prayed for the death of one of our prominent vivisectors, and that the targeted individual always died. This is what M. C. happened to overhear during a conversation at a hotel dinner. After reflecting on this, M. C. continues by saying that they decided to pray that the person most likely to cause suffering to innocent test subjects through their experiments might be taken away, and the result was that approximately two weeks later, one of our most distinguished medical scientists passed away.

I don't know who this scientist was; I imagine some of you might recognize the name. But that's what the Daily Mail reported, and it also mentioned that the Anti-Vivisection Societies were united in condemning this letter, which was entirely appropriate. Now you can see that whoever sent that letter clearly believed he was accomplishing something very worthwhile. I'm certainly no supporter of vivisection myself. I don't believe anyone can truly understand the facts and still support it, but I definitely agreed with the Anti-Vivisection Societies in condemning that kind of letter. You see, there's this assumption that prayer, or mental power, can be used to eliminate someone from life, and M. C. claims that he actually did this in the case of this specific scientist.

That reminds us of another parallel situation, almost what I would call a historical parallel: the case of Dr. Anna Kingsford, which occurred roughly forty years ago. She claimed—and she was indeed a passionate opponent of animal experimentation—that through the power of her thoughts alone, she caused the death of Claude Bernard, France's renowned vivisection scientist. It's true that he died at the exact time she directed her mental forces against him, but it's also been noted that from that very moment, her own decline began and continued relentlessly until she herself passed into the next world. This shows us that such actions are likely to return to those who send them out, even when they achieve their intended result.

In both of these situations, the final goal wasn't a selfish one— it was meant to help humanity and protect animals who cannot speak for themselves. However, this doesn't make the methods acceptable. The saying "The end justifies the means" represents one of the worst distortions of truth, and this becomes even more problematic when this hidden force—the power of suggestion—is used to harm someone for reasons that are more personal than the examples I've mentioned. The more selfish the motivation, the more degraded the action becomes, and it's a serious error to think that using mental techniques somehow changes the fundamental nature of what you're doing.

It has sometimes been my difficult responsibility to sentence individuals to death for murder, and therefore I maintain that I possess extensive knowledge of what distinguishes murder from other instances where life is taken that do not constitute murder; and drawing from my judicial experience spanning many years, along with presiding over numerous cases that involved determining whether the death penalty should be imposed or not, I have no doubt in stating that killing through psychological methods is equally murder as killing by poison or knife. From a judicial standpoint, I would have absolutely no hesitation in executing anyone who committed murder through mental suggestion. Psychological crime, understand, remains crime nonetheless; perhaps it represents an even more heinous form of crime, given the superior knowledge that must accompany it. I assert that the psychological criminal is more dangerous than the conventional criminal.

One of the Master's teachings addresses this exact point. I'm referring to the miracle of the fig tree. You know that he demonstrated his power by killing not a person, not even an animal, but a tree. When the disciples said to him, "Look how this tree you cursed has withered away," he responded, "Well, you can do exactly the same thing," and continued by saying, "Nothing shall be impossible to you." So if you can kill fig trees, you can kill people, but instead, "forgive, if you have anything against anyone," so that your heavenly Father may forgive you.

He essentially says: now that you have witnessed how this hidden power can destroy life, you use it for any other purpose than as a Divine power at your own risk. Use it with prayer to God and with forgiveness toward everyone against whom you hold any kind of resentment or negative feelings, and if you always begin using it in this manner, following the Master's instructions, then no one can use it to harm another person in mind, body, or possessions.

Perhaps some of you might be tempted to smile when I use the word "sorcery," but today, whether we call it by scientific or semi-scientific names, it's really just the ancient practice of sorcery attempting to establish itself among us as a hidden force. Sorcery represents the corrupted application of spiritual power. That's how I define it, and I speak with authority on this matter. I direct you to the Bible, where you'll discover that sorcery holds a prominent position among those things that prevent entry into the heavenly Jerusalem; the heavenly Jerusalem isn't a physical town or city located in any particular place, but rather represents humanity's perfected state. Therefore, if you practice sorcery, you cannot achieve that heavenly condition.

This is why we discover in Revelations that remarkable portrayal of two symbolic women; they embody two different ways the individual soul can express itself. Naturally, they extend beyond this, pointing to national matters, racial development and similar concepts. What's the reason for this? Because every national movement, every racial evolution, has its foundation in the growth of the individual person. A nation or race is simply a group of individuals, so when a principle begins to spread from one person to another, it extends to the entire nation, it reaches the whole race. Therefore, these two symbolic women primarily represent two different soul expressions, two different ways of thinking. You're completely familiar with how these two women are described. The first is the woman dressed in sunlight, standing with the moon beneath her feet, wearing a crown of stars around her head; the second sits on an earthly throne, grasping a golden cup filled with disgusting things. These are the two women, and we understand that Scripture calls one of them Babylon, and we know which one that refers to. One characteristic of this woman—remember this represents a type of personality—is the characteristic of witchcraft, the characteristic of using spiritual and mental abilities in reverse.

But what is the end result? The outcome is that this Babylon becomes a dwelling place for demons, a stronghold—or, as the original Greek text puts it, a prison of evil, an unclean spirit, a cage for every unclean bird. This is the progression that occurs in each person who begins to misuse this mental power. The misuse might start very small, perhaps like what is taught in a certain school that I'm told exists in London, where shop assistants learn to use magnetic power to trick or force unsuspecting customers into buying things they don't want. I'm told such a school exists, though I cannot give you my source. This seems like a minor thing. I walk into a shop and spend two or three shillings buying something that, when I get home, turns out to be completely useless, and I wonder, "How on earth did I end up buying this junk?" Well, I must have been hypnotized into it. It doesn't affect me much, but it makes a huge difference to the young man or woman who hypnotized me, because it represents the first step down a dangerous path. It might involve only sixpence, but it leads from one step to the next, and unless that path is reversed, the final destination is that of Babylon. This is why St. John declares, "I heard a voice from Heaven saying, 'Come forth, my people, out of her'"—meaning out of Babylon—"come forth, my people, out of her"—that is, out of this twisted way of using spiritual power— "come forth, my people, out of her, so that you have no part in her sins and so that you will not receive her punishment." Therefore, I warn everyone against this perverted use of hidden power from the very first day they begin to realize that there exists such a thing as mental or spiritual power that can be used on other people.

Should we then live in constant fear of suffering from harmful mental influence, worrying that some enemy here or there is directing this hidden power against us? If that were the case, we would live in perpetual anxiety. No, I don't believe there's any reason for us to fear in this manner. First of all, relatively few people understand the law of suggestion well enough to use it either positively or negatively, and among those who do understand it sufficiently to apply it, I'm convinced that the majority would only want to use it with good intentions and for the benefit of the person involved. That, I'm certain, is the approach of nine-tenths, or perhaps even ninety-nine percent, of those who study this subject. They want to do good and view their use of mental power as an additional way to help others. But ultimately, human nature is human nature, and there remains a small minority who are both capable and willing to use this hidden power harmfully for their own selfish purposes.

Now how should we handle this minority? The answer is straightforward. Simply see them as they truly are, recognize them for what they actually represent—people who lack genuine spiritual power. They believe they possess it, but they don't. That's the reality of the situation. When you see them in their true light, their influence over you will disappear. The real and ultimate power belongs to the affirmative; the negative destroys, while the affirmative creates. Therefore, this negative misuse of hidden power must be overcome through the use of affirmative, constructive energy. The affirmative always defeats the negative in one specific way, and that's not by confronting it directly, not by charging at it recklessly like a bull in a china shop; instead, it works by building up life. It's always a creative force—constantly building, building, building life and more life, and when that life energy enters, the negative naturally disappears.

The highest positive stance is achieving conscious unity with the source of all life. Once you understand this, you won't need to worry about any negative influences whatsoever. Strive for conscious connection with the ultimate reality, the first cause, which serves as the origin of everything, whether in the cosmos or within you as an individual. This origin is eternally present; it remains constant yesterday, today, and forever, and you represent the world and universe in miniature form, with this force continuously operating within you if you choose to acknowledge it. Keep in mind the mutual relationship between yourself and this genuinely hidden power. While the power of suggestion operates as a concealed force, the power that brings all things into existence is the hidden power that stands behind everything. Now understand that this power exists within you, and you no longer need to concern yourself with negativity. This represents the biblical teaching about Christ; this teaching aims to establish conscious personal unity with the Divine All-creating Spirit as a present living force to be applied in daily life.

The Bible teaches us that there exists something called the mystery of iniquity, which refers to the mystery of spiritual power being used in reverse, employed from a diabolical perspective; and when the Bible speaks of the mystery of iniquity, it means exactly what it states. It tells us that there are powers and principalities in the unseen world that are utilizing precisely these same methods on a massive scale; because, keep in mind one thing, there is never any deviation in any part of the Universe from the universal rule of law; what is law on earth is law in Heaven, law in Hell, law in the invisible and law in the visible; that never changes. What is accomplished by any spiritual power, whether it is a spiritual power of evil or of good, is accomplished through the mental framework that you possess. No power changes the law of your own mind, but a power that understands the law of your mind can utilize it.

Therefore, it's absolutely crucial that you understand how your mind works and recognize that it's constantly open to suggestion. Given this reality, the most important thing is to establish a standard for fundamental, unchangeable, and complete suggestion that you can always rely on—one that becomes so deeply embedded in your subconscious mind that no opposing suggestion can ever replace it. This standard is the mystery of Christ, the Son of God. This is precisely why we learn about the mystery of Christ, the mystery of godliness standing against the mystery of iniquity. Both the divine mystery and the diabolical mystery are trying to work through you, and they can only accomplish this through the natural law of your mental makeup—specifically, through your subconscious mind acting and reacting upon your conscious mind, your body, and ultimately your circumstances.

The mystery of Christ is not simply a religious invention. People have twisted and obscured it by attempting to explain what was not properly understood at that time, by trying to clarify what they did not comprehend; because what we commonly understand today about the laws of the mind was unknown back then. But now that this understanding has emerged, we begin to recognize that the biblical teachings about Christ carry profound and significant meaning, and this is why St. Paul told the Corinthians: "Little children of whom I travail again in birth, until Christ be formed in you." This is why he speaks of "Christ in you the hope of glory," meaning that the Christ concept, the understanding of the Christ principle as demonstrated in the Christ person, connects you with the personal aspect within the Universal Spirit, the divine creative, first moving Spirit of the Universe.

When you recognize this as your basic truth, it becomes continuously embedded in your subconscious mind, even during moments when you're not actively thinking about it, because this is how the subconscious mind operates—it absorbs information and processes it through its own logical reasoning about things you're not consciously considering at the time. This is why understanding that great promise of redemption, which forms the foundation of the Bible from the first chapter of Genesis to the last chapter of Revelation, follows a scientific principle. It's not some magical trick, it's not something that was set up this way but could have easily been arranged differently; it's not this way because some arbitrary Authority decreed it, when that Authority could have just as easily decreed it another way.

No, this is the case because the deeper you investigate it, the more you'll discover that it's completely scientific; it's founded on the natural structure of the human mind. This is why "Christ," as presented in the Bible—whether through Old Testament symbolism or New Testament personality—"fulfills the law," in the sense of developing to the highest degree what is universal to all humanity. As we understand this more fully and develop it more completely, we will ascend to higher levels of communion and greater awareness of mutual identity, shared life with the Universal Power, which will elevate us beyond any possibility of being affected by any form of harmful influence.

If anyone should be so hostile toward us and so sadly lacking in understanding of spiritual truth that they try to use the power of harmful suggestion against us, I feel sorry for the person who attempts to do this. They will gain nothing from it, because they are shooting peas from a toy gun at an armored battleship. That is what it comes down to; but for them it means something more serious. It is a true saying that "Curses return home to roost." I believe if we examine these matters, and recognize that there is a reason for them, we need not be worried in the slightest about negative suggestion, or harmful influence, of falling under the control of other people's minds, of being manipulated in some way, of being cheated out of our possessions, of being harmed in our health, or being damaged in our circumstances, and so forth.

Of course, if you expose yourself to that kind of thing, you will experience it. "Knock, and it shall be opened unto you." This is why Scripture tells us, "He that breaketh through a hedge, a serpent shall bite him." This refers to the serpent that some of us are familiar with—our ancient enemy Nahash. Some of you, at least, have enough training in the inner sciences to recognize the serpent Nahash. Tear down the hedge, meaning the conscious control of your own mind, and especially the hedge of Divine love and wisdom that God himself surrounds you with through the personality of His Son—break down this protective barrier and naturally Nahash enters. However, if you maintain your hedge intact—and remember that the old Hebrew tradition always referred to the Divine Law as "the hedge"—if you keep your hedge whole, nothing can enter except through the door. Christ declared, "I am the door, by me if any man enter in, he shall be saved."

I have discussed the two great mysteries: the mystery of godliness and the mystery of iniquity, the mystery of Christ and the mystery of anti-Christ. Now, you don't need to fully understand these mysteries to find your proper place. If we had to completely grasp these mysteries to either escape from one or enter into the other, I believe we would all face extremely poor odds. I certainly would. I can only touch the surface of these matters, but we can recognize the positive principle and the negative principle that form their foundation; one represents the mystery of light, while the other represents the mystery of darkness.

I'm not saying you shouldn't study these mysteries; they are precisely what we should be studying, but don't think that you stay in a dangerous situation until you have fully understood the mystery. Not at all. You can definitely get on the right track without grasping the entire concept, just like you can travel by train without understanding how the engine that carries you actually works.

So we have these two mysteries—the mystery of light and the mystery of darkness—and what we need to do is choose to receive the mystery of light. When we do this, it will create a center within our own hearts and beings, and we will become aware of that center. Whether we understand it or not, we will become conscious of it. From that center—that center of light within ourselves—we can begin everything in our lives, whether spiritual or worldly. We don't need to go any further back in our search; we don't need to analyze the reasons and explanations behind these things to find our starting point. It might interest us later, and doing so might strengthen us afterward, but for a practical beginning we must recognize the Divine presence within ourselves, which is the son of God revealed in us—the Divine principle of personality speaking from within.

So then, once you've recognized this as your foundation, you carry this all-creating positive force with you through everything you do and everything you are; day and night it will be present, it will protect you, it will guide you, it will help you. And whenever you choose to consciously connect with it, it will provide you with support, and because you use this as your foundation, it will express itself in all your circumstances; because, remember, it is a very simple principle of logic that whatever you begin with will express itself throughout the entire sequence that flows from it. If you begin with the color red you can create all kinds of variations and produce orange, purple and brown, but the red foundation will reveal itself throughout the entire range of color, and similarly if you begin with a foundation of blue, blue will reveal itself throughout the entire spectrum of various colors.

Therefore, if you begin with the positive foundation, the single starting point of the Divine spirit, not taking it from further downstream, but going directly to the source, that positive principle of life will flow throughout everything, revealing its own nature to the very tips of your fingers and beyond that into all your circumstances. So the divine presence will be continuously with you, not as a result of joining this church or that one, following this idea or that teacher, but because you know the truth for yourself, and you have realized it as an actual living experience in your own mind and in your own heart; and therefore it is that this personal recognition of the Divine love and wisdom and power is what St. Paul calls "Christ in you, the hope of glory."

Everyone who recognizes this truth is someone who fits the Biblical description of a genuine Israelite. The word "Israelite" in the Bible carries deep symbolic meaning and holds tremendous significance. So embrace this recognition as a practical reality that each of you is truly an Israelite, and if this is the case, then find complete joy in the eternal declaration that remains as true today as it was when first spoken: "There is no divination or enchantment against Israel."

III: The "I Am"

We often fail to fully appreciate the wisdom in Walt Whitman's insightful observation, "I am not all contained between my hat and my boots," and we overlook the dual nature of the "I AM"—that it exists simultaneously as both the manifested and the unmanifested, the universal and the individual. When we lose sight of this fundamental truth, we create limitations around ourselves; we perceive only a fragment of the self, and then we're puzzled when that fragment cannot accomplish the work of the complete whole. Unexpected elements emerge that we hadn't anticipated, and we question their origins, failing to understand that they inevitably spring from that vast unity that encompasses us all.

It is the magnificent intelligence and vitality of Universal Spirit constantly pushing forward to express itself through a glorious humanity.

This can only be achieved when each person recognizes their ability to work together with the Supreme Principle through an intelligent understanding of its purpose and the natural laws that accomplish that purpose—a recognition that can only come from realizing that they themselves are nothing other than the same Universal Principle expressed in a specific form.

When he realizes this, he understands that Walt Whitman's words ring true, and that his source of intelligence, power, and purpose lies within that Universal Self, which belongs to him just as much as it belongs to anyone else precisely because it is universal, and which is therefore as fully and completely one with himself as if no other expression of it existed anywhere in the world.

The understanding that truly gives meaning to knowledge is recognizing that when we use the formula "I am, therefore I can, therefore I will," the "I AM" that begins this sequence represents a being who essentially has their head in heaven and their feet on earth—a complete unity with a scope of ideas that far exceeds the small thoughts limited by what a single day or hour demands. At the same time, the needs of each day and hour are genuine while they exist, and since our expressed life can only be lived in the present moment, whether that's today or ten thousand years from now, what we need is to bring harmony between our life of expression and our life of purpose, and by discovering within ourselves the source of our highest purposes, we also discover the life of our fullest expression.

This is the meaning of prayer. Prayer isn't a foolish attempt to change the mind of Supreme Wisdom, but rather an intelligent effort to embody that wisdom in our thoughts so we can express it more and more perfectly when we express ourselves. Therefore, as we gradually develop the habit of discovering this inspiring Presence within ourselves, and of recognizing its forward movement as the ultimate determining factor in all true healthful mental action, it will become second nature to us to have all our plans, down to the seemingly most trivial ones, floating upon the undercurrent of this Universal Intelligence so that a great harmony will enter our lives, every discordant manifestation will vanish, and we shall find ourselves increasingly controlling all things into the forms that we desire.

Why? Is it because we've learned to control the Spirit and force it to obey us? Absolutely not, for "if the blind lead the blind both shall fall into the ditch"; rather, it's because we've become partners with the Spirit, and through ongoing and deepening intimacy we've transformed not "the mind of the Spirit," but our own minds, and we've discovered how to think from an elevated perspective, where we understand that the ancient wisdom "know thyself" encompasses the knowledge of everything we mean when we speak of God.

I AM IS ONE

This might appear to be a very basic idea, but it's one that we tend to forget all too easily. What does this actually mean? It means everything; however, we're primarily interested in what it means for us personally, and for each individual it signifies this. It signifies that there aren't two separate Spirits—one that represents me and another that represents someone else. It signifies that there isn't some vast unknown force outside of myself that might be driven by completely different motivations than mine, and which would therefore confront me with its overwhelming power and steamroll right over me, leaving me crushed and shattered like a worshipper who gets run over by the chariot of Jagannath. It signifies that there exists only one mind, one motivation, one power—not two forces working against each other—and that my conscious mind in all its activities is simply this one mind expressing itself as (not just working through) my own unique individuality.

There is only one I AM, not two separate ones. Whatever I can imagine the Great Universal Life Principle to be, that is what I am. Let's try to fully understand what this means. Can you imagine the Great Originating and Sustaining Life Principle of the entire universe as poor, weak, corrupt, miserable, jealous, angry, worried, uncertain, or limited in any other way? We know this is impossible. Since the I AM is one, it is equally false to think of ourselves this way. First learn to distinguish your true self from the mental and physical processes that it projects as tools for its expression, and then understand that this self controls these tools, not the other way around. As we grow in this understanding, we recognize ourselves as unlimited, and that in the small world where we are the center, we ourselves are the same overflowing of joyful life energy that the Great Life Spirit is in the Great All. The I AM is One.

IV: Affirmative Power

To fully understand the true nature of positive power is to hold the key to the greatest secret. We sense its presence in all the countless forms of life that surround us, and we feel it as the life force within ourselves. Eventually, one day the truth strikes us like a revelation—that we can control this power, this life force, through the process of thought. As soon as we recognize this, we begin to understand how important it is to control our thinking. We start asking ourselves what this thought process actually is, and we discover that it involves directing positive force into forms that are created by our own thoughts. We mentally create the form in our minds and then breathe life into it through our thinking.

This must always be the nature of the creative process at any level, whether on the vast scale of the Universal Cosmic Mind or on the smaller scale of the individual mind; the difference lies only in degree and not in kind. We can visualize the mental mechanisms through which this occurs in whatever way best satisfies our understanding—and satisfying our understanding on this matter is a powerful factor in giving us that confidence in our mental activity without which we cannot accomplish anything—but the actual manifestation results from something more powerful than mere intellectual comprehension. It stems from that inner mental state which, for lack of a better term, we might call our emotional understanding of ourselves. It is the "self" that we feel ourselves to be that takes on forms of our own creation. For this reason our thinking must be so firmly based on knowledge that we will feel the truth of it, and thus be able to create within ourselves that mental attitude of feeling which matches the condition we wish to manifest.

We cannot think into existence a different kind of life than what we actually experience within ourselves. As Horace says, "Nemo dat quod non habet," we cannot give what we do not possess. And conversely, we can never stop creating forms of some kind through our mental activity, breathing life into them through our thoughts. This point must be very carefully understood. We cannot remain idle and produce nothing: our mental machinery will continue operating and producing work of some kind, and it is up to us to decide what kind it will be. In our complete ignorance or incomplete understanding of this principle, we create negative forms and breathe life into them through our thinking. We create forms of death, illness, sadness, trouble, and limitations of every kind, and then give life to these forms through our thoughts; the result is that, although they have no real existence in themselves, they become realities to us and cast their shadow across the path that would otherwise be bright with the multicolored beauty of countless flowers and the glory of sunshine.

This doesn't have to be the case. We're giving negative thoughts a positive power that they don't actually possess. Think about what negative really means. It represents the absence of something. It's non-existence, and it lacks everything that makes up actual existence. When left alone, it stays in its own emptiness, and it only takes shape and becomes active when we give it these qualities through our thinking.

Here, then, is the main reason for practicing control over our thoughts. It is the only tool we have to work with, but it is a tool that works with complete certainty, creating limitation if we think limitation, creating expansion if we think expansion. Our thought as feeling is the magnet that attracts to us those conditions that precisely match itself. This is what is meant by the saying that "thoughts are things." But, you ask, how can I think differently from my circumstances? Certainly you are not expected to say that the circumstances at this moment are what they are not; to say so would be false; but what is needed is not to think from the perspective of circumstances at all. Think from that inner perspective where there are no circumstances, and from where you can determine what circumstances will be, and then let the circumstances take care of themselves.

Do not focus on specific circumstances like particular aspects of health, peace, or other conditions, but rather concentrate on health, peace, and prosperity as complete concepts. Here is an advertisement from Pearson's Weekly: "Think money. Big moneymakers think money." This represents a perfectly accurate description of thought's power, even though it appears in an advertisement; however, we can progress beyond simply thinking about "money." We can think about "Life" in its complete fullness, along with that perfect harmony of conditions which encompasses everything we need in terms of money and countless other beneficial things as well, some of which money represents as a symbol of exchangeable value, while others cannot be measured by such a material standard.

Therefore, focus your thoughts on Life, illumination, harmony, prosperity, and happiness—concentrate on these essential qualities rather than specific circumstances or conditions related to them. Through the reliable workings of the Universal Law, these qualities will naturally shape themselves into forms that are perfectly suited to your unique situation, and they will become part of your life as dynamic, living energies that will remain with you permanently because you understand them to be fundamental aspects of your own existence.

V: Submission

There are two types of submission: giving in to superior force and yielding to superior truth. One represents weakness while the other demonstrates strength. Learning to tell these two apart forms an extremely important part of our development, especially since most popular religious teachings today wrongly praise the first type as the highest form of human achievement. Some people take this so far that it becomes a tool for actual oppression, and for everyone it creates weakness and blocks progress. We're told not to question what are called the wise plans of Providence and are instructed that pain and suffering should be accepted because they represent God's will; there's plenty of eloquent speaking and writing about the beauty of quiet acceptance, all of which appeals to certain gentle souls who haven't yet learned that true gentleness doesn't come from lacking power but from using it with kindness and for good purposes.

People with this type of mindset are especially prone to being deceived. They see a certain beauty in the image of weakness depending on strength, but they misidentify what makes this combination so appealing. A careful examination would reveal that their emotions are made up of sympathy for the weak person and respect for the strong one, and that the power of the entire scene comes from how it satisfies our artistic need for balance, which demands this kind of contrast. But which of the two people in this scene would they actually want to be? Certainly not the weak person who needs assistance, but the strong person who provides it. On its own, the weak person only awakens our sympathy, not our respect. Their appearance might be beautiful, but this very beauty only emphasizes the sense that something is missing—and what's missing is strength. The appeal that the philosophy of passive acceptance has for certain people is built on an emotional argument that is accepted without any doubt that the emotion being targeted is a misleading one.

The beneficial impact of the movement called "The Higher Thought" lies exactly in this—it dedicates itself strictly to fighting against this weakening philosophy of surrender. It can recognize just as clearly as others the appeal of frailty depending on power; however, it understands that the genuine foundation of this appeal rests in the powerful component of the pairing. The authentic beauty exists in the ability to give strength, and this ability cannot be gained through surrender, but through the completely opposite approach of constantly declaring our resolve not to give in.

Of course, if we assume that all the sadness, illness, pain, hardship, and other difficulties in the world represent God's will, then we certainly must accept what cannot be changed with complete submission, and find comfort in the uncertain hope that somehow in some distant future we will discover that

"Good is the ultimate purpose of suffering."

though even this vague hope is a protest against the very submission we are endeavoring to exercise. But to make the assumption that the evil of life is the will of God is to assume what a careful and intelligent study of the laws of the universe, both mental and physical, will show us is not the truth; and if we turn to that Book which contains the fullest delineation of these universal laws, we shall find nothing taught more clearly than that submission to the evils of life is not submission to the will of God. We are told that Christ was manifested for this end, that he should destroy him that has the power of death—that is, the devil. Now death is the very culmination of the Negative. It is the entire absence of all that makes Life, and whatever goes to diminish the living quality of Life reproduces, in its degree, the distinctive quality of this supreme exhibition of the Negative. Everything that tends to detract from the fullness of life has in it this deathful quality.

In that completely transformed life, which is represented by the symbol of the New Jerusalem, we are told that sorrow and sighing will disappear, and that no resident will say, I am sick. Nothing that clouds life, or limits it, can come from the same source as the Power that brings light to those who sit in darkness, and freedom to those who are imprisoned. Negation can never become Affirmation; and the mistake we must always protect ourselves against is attributing positive power to the Negative. Once we understand the truth that God is life, and that life in every form of expression can never be anything other than Affirmative, then it must become obvious to us that nothing which has the opposite tendency can be in accordance with God's will. For God (the good) to desire any of the "evil" that exists in the world would be for Life to act with the intention of reducing itself, which contradicts the very concept of Life. God is Life, and Life is, by its essential nature, Affirmative. The surrender we have made up to this point has been to our own weakness, ignorance, and fear, and not to the supreme good.

But is there no such thing as submission required of us under any circumstances? Are we always supposed to have our own way in everything? The entire secret of our progress toward freedom lies in developing the habit of submission, but this means submitting to higher Truth, not to superior force. Sometimes, when we reach a higher Truth, we discover that accepting it requires us to reorganize the truths we already possessed. We don't need to discard any of them, because once we recognize Truth, we can never lose sight of it again. However, we must recognize a different relationship between these truths than we saw before. Then comes the process of submitting what has been our highest truth to one we recognize as even higher. This process isn't always easy to achieve, but we must go through it if we want our spiritual development to continue. The smaller degree of life must be absorbed into the greater one. For this to happen, we need to learn that the smaller degree was only a partial and limited view of something more universal, stronger, and larger in every way.

Now, as we go through the processes of spiritual growth, there's plenty of opportunity for that training in self-knowledge and self-control which is commonly understood by the word "submission." However, the nature of this act is fundamentally changed. It's no longer a half-despairing resignation to a superior force outside ourselves, which we can only vaguely hope is acting with kindness and wisdom, but rather it becomes an intelligent recognition of the true nature of our own inner forces and of the laws by which a strong spiritual constitution is to be developed; and the submission is no longer to limitations which drain life of its vitality, and against which we naturally rebel, but to the law of our own evolution which shows itself in continuously increasing degrees of life and strength.

The surrender we acknowledge is the cost that must be paid for growth in any area. Even in financial markets, we must invest before we can earn returns. It is a universal law that Nature responds to us precisely to the degree that we first follow Nature's ways; and this applies equally to spiritual understanding as it does to physical matters. The only question is whether we will give blind submission to the principle of Death, or offer willing and thoughtful obedience to the principle of Life.

If we have clearly understood the reality of our oneness with Universal Spirit, we will discover that, when moving in the right direction, there is truly no such thing as submission. Submission involves yielding to the power of another—a person cannot be said to submit to themselves. When the "I AM" within us recognizes a greater level of I AM-ness (if I may create this term) than it has previously achieved, then, through the very power of this recognition, it becomes what it perceives, and therefore naturally releases from itself whatever would restrict its expression of its own wholeness.

But this represents a natural growth process, not an unnatural act of surrender; it isn't about pouring ourselves out in weakness, but rather about gathering ourselves together with growing strength. Spirit contains no weakness—it is pure strength—and we must therefore remain constantly alert to the subtle advances of the Negative, which seeks to reverse the true situation. The Negative always points toward some external source of power. Its formula is "I AM NOT." It consistently attempts to create a divide between us and the Infinite Sufficiency. It would always have us believe that this sufficiency doesn't belong to us, but that through some uncertain favor we might receive occasional portions of it handed out to us. Christ's teaching differs from this. We don't need to come with our pitcher to the well to draw water, like the woman of Samaria, but we carry within ourselves an inexhaustible supply of the living water springing up into everlasting life.

Let us write "No Surrender" in bold letters on our banner, and move forward fearlessly to claim our rightful inheritance of freedom and life.

VI: Completeness

A point that students of mental science often fail to emphasize enough is the wholeness of humanity—not a wholeness to be achieved in the future, but right here and now. We have become so used to having human imperfection constantly reinforced through books, sermons, and hymns, and most importantly through a misguided interpretation of the Bible, that initially the concept of human completeness completely overwhelms us. However, until we grasp this truth, we will remain excluded from the highest and finest offerings of mental science, from a complete understanding of its philosophy, and from its most significant practical accomplishments.

To accomplish any task successfully, you must believe that you are fully capable of handling it. The finished work reflects a corresponding sense of wholeness within yourself. If this principle applies to one task, it applies to all tasks; the significance of the work doesn't change this truth. We cannot successfully undertake any project until we somehow believe we can achieve it. In other words, we must believe that we possess all the necessary qualities for completion and that we are therefore complete in our ability to handle it. Recognizing our own completeness determines what we can accomplish, which is why understanding the reality of our own wholeness is so important.

But someone might ask, don't we see imperfection everywhere around us? Isn't there sadness, illness, and hardship? Yes, there is;

but why does this happen? It's precisely because we don't recognize our own wholeness. If we truly understood this completeness, these problems wouldn't exist; and as we gradually come to understand it, we'll see these difficulties steadily fade away. Now if we truly understand the two basic truths that Spirit is pure Life itself, and that external circumstances result from inner forces, then it shouldn't be hard to see why we should be whole; because to think otherwise would mean assuming that the universe's creative power is either unable or unwilling to fully express its own purpose in creating humanity.

That it would be unable to do so would remove it from its position as the creative principle, and that it would be unwilling to fulfill its own purpose is a contradiction; so either way we reach an impossible conclusion. When creating humanity, the creative principle must have therefore produced a perfect work, and our view of ourselves as flawed can only result from our own lack of understanding about what we truly are; and our progress, therefore, doesn't involve having something new added to us, but rather learning to activate powers that already exist within us, but which we have never attempted to use, and therefore have not developed, simply because we have always assumed that we are naturally lacking in some of the most essential abilities needed to adapt us to our surroundings.

If we want to achieve these great powers, the question becomes: where should we look for them? The answer lies within ourselves. This is the great secret. We shouldn't search outside ourselves for power. The moment we do this, we discover not power, but weakness. To look for strength from any external source is to declare our own weakness, and everyone knows what the inevitable result of such a declaration must be.

We are whole and complete within ourselves; the reason we don't realize this truth is that we don't understand how far our "self" actually reaches. We understand that anything whole is made up of all its parts, not just some of them; yet somehow we don't seem to grasp this concept when it comes to ourselves. We correctly say that every person represents a focused concentration of the Universal Spirit expressed as individual consciousness; but if this is true, then each individual consciousness must discover that the Universal Spirit is the infinite expression of itself. This is the part of our "Self" that we so frequently overlook when we evaluate who we are; as a result, we see ourselves as insignificant, crawling creatures when we could view ourselves as powerful archangels. We attempt to work with nothing more than pale shadows of our true selves instead of embracing our magnificent essence, and then we're surprised when we fail. If we could only grasp that our "better half" is the entire infinite realm of Spirit— the very force that creates and maintains the universe—then we would truly understand just how complete our wholeness really is.

As we come to understand this idea, our wholeness becomes real to us, and we discover that we don't need to look beyond ourselves for anything. We simply need to tap into that part of ourselves that is infinite to fulfill any purpose we might create in our individual awareness; there is no wall between these two aspects, or they wouldn't form a complete whole. Each part belongs entirely to the other, and together they are one. There is no conflict between them, because the Infinite Life cannot have any interest that opposes its own individualization of itself. If we experience any sense of strain, it comes from not fully grasping this understanding of our own completeness; we are creating a barrier somewhere when in reality there isn't one; and this strain will persist until we discover where and how we are building this barrier and eliminate it.

This feeling of tension arises because we're not utilizing our complete being. We're attempting to make half of ourselves do the work that requires our entirety; however, we cannot escape our wholeness, and consequently our complete self rebels against our efforts to pit one half against the other. When we understand that our focus from the Infinite also means our expansion into it, we'll recognize that our entire "self" encompasses both the concentration and the expansion; and grasping this concept intellectually first, we'll gradually learn to apply our understanding practically and bring our complete being to whatever task we undertake. We'll discover that within us there exists a continuous action and reaction between the infinite and the individual, similar to blood circulation flowing from the heart to the extremities and returning again, a steady pulsation of vital energy that is completely natural and free from any strain or effort.

This is the great secret of Life's vitality, and it goes by many names and is expressed through various symbols across different religions and philosophies, each having value to the extent that it brings us closer to understanding this perfect completeness. However, the essence itself is Life, and therefore can only be hinted at, never fully captured, by any words or symbols; it is a personal experience that no one can share with another. All we can do is show the direction where this experience can be found, and share the logical reasoning that has helped us discover it; but the experience itself involves the functioning of specific vital aspects of our inner being, and no one else can live our life for us.

However, as much as we can put these concepts into words, what happens when we truly understand that our "self" contains both the Infinite and the Individual? We gain access to all the resources of the Infinite; we can use them however we choose, and the only restriction comes from the Law of Kindness—a limit we place on ourselves, which isn't slavery but simply another way our freedom shows itself. In this way, we become truly free with all restrictions lifted.

We are no longer ignorant, because the "self" within us contains the Infinite, allowing us to access all the knowledge we need. While we might not always be able to express this knowledge through our rational mind, we will sense its direction, and eventually our thinking will learn to put this understanding into words as well. By combining thought with experience and theory with practice, we will gradually gain deeper insight into the Law of our Being, discovering that fear has no place within it, since it operates as the law of perfect freedom. Understanding what our complete self truly is, we will stand tall as free individuals, radiating Light and Life in all directions, so that our mere presence carries a life-giving influence, because we recognize ourselves as a positive, unified Whole rather than just a negative collection of disconnected pieces.

We understand that our complete self encompasses that Greater Being which exists behind and creates the physical person, and this Greater Being represents the authentic human essence within us. This essence is therefore universal in its understanding, while simultaneously remaining uniquely and individually ourselves; consequently, the genuine person within us, being both universal and individual at once, can be relied upon as a dependable guide. This is the "Thinker" that exists beyond our conscious mind, and when we accept it as our center and recognize that it is not a separate being but ourselves, it will prove capable of handling every situation and will guide us from a state of bondage into "the glorious liberty of the sons of God."

VII: The Principle of Guidance

If I were asked which spiritual principle ranks first among all others, I would be inclined to say the Principle of Guidance. This isn't because it's more essential than the rest, since every part is equally vital to creating a complete and perfect whole. Rather, it comes first in the natural order of things and gives meaning to all our other abilities by putting them in proper relationship with each other. I say it "gives meaning to our other abilities" because guidance itself is one of our powers. From the perspective of our personal self-awareness, this principle appears to be above us. However, when we understand it from the viewpoint of the unity of all Spirit, we realize it's actually part of ourselves. This is because it represents that Infinite Mind which must necessarily be one with all its expressions.

Looking to this Infinite Mind as a higher intelligence from which we can receive guidance doesn't mean we're seeking help from an outside source. Instead, we're turning to the deepest wellspring of our own existence, trusting in its power so completely that we can move forward with our plans with unwavering confidence and certainty—qualities that are themselves the very foundation of our success.

The spiritual principles working within us follow the order that we establish through our thoughts; therefore, the sequence of manifestation will mirror the sequence of our desires; and if we ignore this fundamental principle of proper order and direction, we will discover ourselves starting to express other great powers that currently lie dormant within us, without understanding how to find appropriate uses for them—which would be an extremely dangerous situation, because without having before us goals worthy of the powers we are awakening, we would squander them on trivial purposes guided only by the limited scope of our unenlightened mind. Therefore the ancient wisdom teaches, "With all thy getting, get understanding."

The awakening to awareness of our mysterious inner powers will eventually happen, and will lead to us using them whether we understand how they develop or not, just as we already use our physical abilities whether we understand their principles or not. The inner powers are natural abilities just as much as the outer ones. We can guide their use by understanding their principles; and it is therefore extremely important to have some reliable foundation for direction in using these higher abilities as they start to show themselves.

If we want to safely and beneficially claim the tremendous inheritance of power that lies ahead of us, we must first work to develop within ourselves that Higher Intelligence which will serve as a reliable guiding principle, provided we acknowledge it as such. Everything hinges on our recognition. Thoughts are real things, and therefore as we direct our thoughts to be, so we direct reality to be. If we choose to employ the Infinite Spirit as a guiding force, we will discover that reality aligns with our intention; and in doing so, we are still utilizing our own highest principle. This represents the true "understanding" which, by arranging all our other abilities in their proper sequence, establishes one magnificent unity of power focused toward clearly defined and noble purposes, rather than the scattering of our abilities, through which they merely cancel each other out and accomplish nothing.

This is the Spirit of Truth that will guide us into all Truth. It represents our genuine desire reaching out toward Truth. Truth must come first, and power should follow afterward—this is the logical sequence that we cannot reverse without harming ourselves and others. However, when we follow this proper order, we will always discover opportunities for our abilities to transform the ever-expanding magnificence of our ideal vision into present-day realities.

The ideal represents what is truly real, but it must be brought into physical reality before this truth can be demonstrated, and this is where the practical aspect of our mental studies lies. The practical mystic is the person who holds real power; this is someone who, recognizing the mystical abilities within themselves, aligns their external actions with this understanding, thereby demonstrating their faith through their deeds; and certainly the first step involves utilizing that power of perfect guidance which they can access simply by wanting to be guided by it.

VIII: Desire as the Driving Force

There are certain Eastern philosophical schools, along with various Western branches that have grown from them, which are built entirely on the principle of destroying all desire. The core of their teaching is this: reach the point where you want nothing at all, and you will discover true freedom. To support this idea, they present a great deal of very convincing arguments, which are particularly likely to trap the unsuspecting, because these arguments acknowledge many of the deepest truths about Nature. However, we must remember that it's possible to have profound knowledge of psychological facts while at the same time corrupting the results of our knowledge through a completely wrong assumption about the law that connects these facts within the universal system. The harmful consequences of misunderstanding such a crucial question are so fundamental and extensive that we cannot emphasize too strongly the need to clearly grasp the true nature of what's at stake. When we strip away all the extras and decorations, the question comes down to this: Which will we choose as our destiny, Life or Death? There can be no compromise between these two options, and whichever we select as our guiding principle must produce results that are characteristic of its own nature.

The entire weight of this crucial question depends on where we place desire within our framework of thinking. Is it the Tree of Life standing at the center of the Garden of the Soul? Or is it the Upas Tree that creates a wasteland of death everywhere around it?

This is the matter on which we must make a decision, and this decision will influence our entire understanding of life and shape the full scope of what we can achieve. Let us therefore attempt to envision the ideal put forward by the philosophies I have mentioned—a person who has completely destroyed all desire within themselves. For such a person, everything must appear identical. Good and evil must seem the same, because nothing retains the ability to awaken any desire in them; they no longer possess any emotion that would lead them to declare, "This is good, so I will choose it; that is evil, so I will turn away from it"; because every choice requires recognizing something more appealing in what we select compared to what we dismiss, and therefore requires the presence of that sense of desire which has been completely removed from the ideal we are examining.

Then, if someone's ability to perceive what makes one thing better than another has been completely wiped out, there can be no reason for taking any kind of action at all. Give a person who has destroyed their capacity for wanting things the power to create an entire universe, and they would have no reason to use that power. Give them complete knowledge, and it would be worthless to them; since they no longer experience desire, they have no purpose for which to put their knowledge to use. And we cannot give them Love, because love is desire at its highest level. But if all of this is taken away, what remains of the person? Nothing except their physical appearance. If someone has actually achieved this ideal state, they have essentially stopped existing as a human being. Nothing can possibly interest them, because there is nothing in one thing rather than another that could attract or repel them. They must be completely dead to all emotion and all reasons for action, because both feeling and action require preferring one situation over another; and when desire has been totally eliminated, no such preference can exist.

Someone might argue that only evil desires should be suppressed this way, but reading the writings from these philosophical schools reveals this isn't true. The entire foundation of their system rests on the idea that all desire must be eliminated—the desire for good things just as much as the desire for bad things. Good is considered just as much of an "illusion" as evil, and we haven't achieved freedom until we reach complete indifference to both. Once we have completely destroyed all desire, we become free. The practical consequences of this philosophy can be seen in Indian devotees who, following their commitment to eliminate all desire for both good and evil, become nothing more than empty shells of human beings, having long ago lost all ability to perceive and act.

The merging with the universal that they strive for becomes nothing more than self-imposed hypnosis, which, when sustained long enough, drains away all mental and physical strength, leaving behind only the empty shell of a weakened human body—the hopeless remains of what was once a living person. This is the inevitable outcome of a philosophy that begins with the assumption that desire is inherently evil, that every desire is fundamentally a form of slavery, regardless of what it seeks. Most followers of this philosophy may not have enough determination to follow it strictly to its logical end; but whether their goal is meant to be achieved in this life or another, the complete elimination of desire means nothing other than total indifference, without emotion and without action.

This idea is completely wrong—not just when we look at our everyday lives, but also when we consider the most elevated understanding of the Universal Principle—and we can see this simply because anything exists at all. If complete indifference were the highest ideal, then the Creative Power of the universe would have to be incredibly crude; and everything we've always seen as the amazing order and beauty of creation would be nothing more than a show of poor taste and ignorance of true philosophy.

But the fact that creation exists proves that the Universal Mind thinks differently, and we only need to look around to see that the true ideal is the exercise of creative power. Therefore, far from desire being something to be destroyed, it is the very foundation of every conceivable form of Life. Without it, Life could not exist. Every form of expression involves choosing all that goes into making up that form, and leaving behind whatever is not needed for that purpose; this means having a desire for what is chosen over what is set aside. And this selective desire is nothing other than the universal Law of Attraction.

Whether this law operates as the chemical attraction between seemingly unconscious atoms, or through the instinctive, though unreasoned, attractions found in the plant and animal kingdoms, it remains the principle of selective affinity; and it continues to function identically when it advances into the higher realms governed by reason and conscious intention. The methods of activity within each of these realms are determined by the nature of that particular realm; but the activity itself always stems from one specific subject's preference for one specific object, while excluding all others; and all action consists of the mutual movement of these two elements toward each other in accordance with the law governing their affinity.

When this occurs within the realm of conscious individuality, these natural attractions manifest themselves as mental activity; however, the principle of selection operates universally without exception throughout the entire universe. In the conscious mind, this attraction toward what naturally belongs with it transforms into desire; the desire to create circumstances that are better than those currently existing. Our lack of knowledge might lead us to make errors about what this better thing truly is, and therefore in attempting to fulfill our desire we might misdirect it; but the problem lies not in the desire itself, but in our mistaken understanding of what it actually needs for its fulfillment. This results in restlessness and dissatisfaction until its true natural partner is discovered; but once this is found, the law of attraction immediately takes effect and creates that improved condition, the vision of which originally guided our thoughts.

Therefore, it remains eternally true that desire serves as the source of all emotion and all action; put differently, it is the foundation of all Life. The complete vitality of Life involves either receiving or sending out the vibrations created by the law of attraction; within the realm of mind, these vibrations inevitably transform into conscious extensions of the mind toward whatever draws its attention; meaning they evolve into desires. Desire represents the mind's attempt to express itself in some form that currently exists only within its thoughts. It functions as the fundamental principle of creation, regardless of whether what is being created is a world or a simple wooden spoon; both originate from the desire to bring something into being that does not yet exist. No matter what level we apply our creative capacity, the driving force will always be desire.

Desire drives everything in existence; it serves as the fundamental force that moves the universe and forms the core essence of all life. Therefore, choosing to reject desire as our basic principle means attempting to eliminate life itself; instead, we need to gain the necessary understanding to direct our desires toward what will truly fulfill them. This represents the ultimate purpose of all knowledge; any knowledge used differently remains incomplete and, having missed its mark, amounts to nothing more than ignorance. Desire encompasses the complete vitality of life, since it generates all movement, whether in the physical realm or the spiritual dimension. Simply put, desire represents the creative force, and we must protect, develop, and channel it with great care; working to cultivate it to its highest potential stands in complete contrast to attempting to destroy it entirely.

Desire naturally leads to fulfillment. Desire and its fulfillment are connected like cause and effect; when we understand how they follow each other, we become even more convinced of how incredibly important Desire is as the central force of Life.

IX: Touching Lightly

What serves as our foundation? Does it come from within ourselves or from external sources? Do we maintain our own stability, or does our equilibrium rely on something outside of us? Our lives will reflect whatever genuine beliefs shape our responses to these questions. In all things, there exist two components: the fundamental and the secondary—the core that gives meaning and purpose to the entire matter, and everything that surrounds this center and derives its shape from it. True understanding always involves separating these two elements from one another, while mistakes always stem from confusing their proper places.

In all our affairs, there are two elements: ourselves and the situation we need to handle. Since our understanding of anything is always shaped by how we think about it, it comes down entirely to our beliefs about which of these two elements should be primary and which should be secondary. Whichever one we consider primary automatically makes the other one secondary. The secondary element can never be completely absent. For any kind of action to happen, there must be certain conditions that allow the activity to manifest into visible outcomes. However, the same type of activity can occur under many different conditions and can therefore produce very different visible outcomes. Therefore, in every situation we will always discover a primary or driving element, and a secondary element that gets its characteristics from the nature of that driving force.

We can never avoid having to choose between what's essential and what's merely incidental, and whatever we pick as essential automatically makes the other incidental. When we make the error of getting this backwards and assume that our driving force comes from secondary circumstances, we end up relying on them for support and depending on them completely, rising or falling based on their whims. This leaves us in a state of weakness and servile dependence on all kinds of outside influences, which is the complete opposite of the strength, wisdom, and abundance that define true Liberty.

But if we ask ourselves the straightforward question: Where can the center of a person's life be except within themselves? we will see that in everything that concerns us, the energizing center must be within ourselves. We can never escape from ourselves as the center of our own universe, and the sooner we clearly grasp this, the better. There is truly no energy in our universe except what flows from ourselves in the first place, and the power that seems to exist in our surroundings comes entirely from our own mind.

Once we understand this truth and recognize that the Life flowing into us from the Universal Life-Principle is completely fresh Life at every moment, entirely undifferentiated for any specific purpose except to sustain our individual existence, and that we therefore have the power to express it in whatever form we choose, we discover that this expression of the eternal Life-Principle within us becomes the foundation from which we can influence our environment. We must rely steadily on the central core of our own existence and not depend on anything external. Our error lies in taking our circumstances too seriously. We should approach things with a lighter touch. The moment we sense that their burden hinders our ability to handle them freely, they are controlling us rather than us controlling them.

Light handling doesn't mean weak handling. In fact, a light touch is incompatible with a weak grip on the instrument, which suggests that the tool's weight is too much for the force trying to control it. A light, even playful approach, therefore requires a firm grip and complete control over the instrument. Only in the hands of a Grinling Gibbons can the carving tool create miracles of weightless beauty from solid wood. The light yet firm touch speaks not of weakness, but of power held in reserve; and when we recognize our own complete spiritual nature we understand that behind any amount of power we may express there is the entire reserve of the infinite to support us.

As we come to understand this, we start to handle situations with a light touch, playing with them like a juggler works with flying knives that can only move exactly as he directs them, because we begin to realize that our control over circumstances is part of the essential order of the universe. The chaos we've encountered before has happened precisely because we never consciously tried to incorporate this aspect of our personal control as part of the overall system.

Of course, I'm talking about the complete person, not just the physical part that Walt Whitman describes as existing between someone's hat and boots. The complete person represents something infinite, and the visible part of them serves as the tool through which they observe and experience everything that belongs to them—their own realm of the infinite. When someone discovers that this is what their conscious individuality truly means, they understand how they can be infinite, and they realize they are united with the Infinite Mind, which forms the deepest essence of the universe. Once they've found this true center of their being, they can never allow anything else to take this central position, but will understand that in relation to this center, everything else exists as secondary and supplementary. As they grow daily in this understanding, they will learn to manage all things with a light yet steady touch, so that sadness, fear, and mistakes will occupy less and less room in their world, until eventually sorrow and grief will disappear completely, and eternal joy will replace them. We may have only taken a few steps along this path so far, but they're moving in the right direction, and what we need to do now is continue forward.

X: Present Truth

If the power of thought is good for anything, it's good for everything. If it can create one thing, it can create all things. What could possibly prevent it? Nothing can stop us from thinking. We can think whatever we want, and if thinking means creating, then we can create whatever we want. The entire question, therefore, comes down to this: Is it true that thinking means creating? If so, don't we see that our limitations are created in exactly the same way as our growth? We think that conditions outside our thoughts have power over us, and so we give them that power through our thinking. So the great question of life is whether there exists any other creative power besides thought. If there is, where is it, and what is it?

Both philosophy and religion guide us to the understanding that "in the beginning" there existed no creative force other than Spirit, and the only form of activity we can assign to Spirit is Thought, which means we discover Thought as the foundation of everything. If this was true "in the beginning," it must remain true now; because if everything originates from Thought, then everything must be expressions of Thought, making it impossible for Spirit to ever transfer its creations to some force that is not itself—meaning something that is not Thought-power; therefore all the shapes and situations that surround us are expressions of the creative power of Thought.

However, someone might argue that this is God's Thought, and that the creative power belongs to God, not to humanity. Yet this argument moves away from the self-evident, fundamental truth that "in the beginning" nothing could have originated except through Thought. It is absolutely true that nothing has any origin except within the Divine Mind, and humanity itself is therefore a form of Divine Thought. Furthermore, humans are self-conscious; therefore, humanity represents Divine Thought that has evolved into individual consciousness, and when a person becomes sufficiently enlightened to recognize this as their origin, they understand that they are an individual reproduction of the same spirit that creates all things, and that their own individual thought possesses exactly the same quality as Divine Thought in its universal form, just as fire remains equally fiery whether it burns around a large center of combustion or a small one, and thus we are logically led to the conclusion that our thought must possess creative power.

But people say, "We haven't experienced this. We're surrounded by all kinds of situations we don't want." Yes, you're afraid of them, and by being afraid you're thinking about them; and this way you're constantly using this Divine gift of creation through Thought, except through ignorance you're using it in the wrong direction. This is why the Book of Divine Instructions so often repeats "Fear not; doubt not," because we can never strip our Thought of its natural creative power, and the only question is whether we'll use it ignorantly to harm ourselves or with understanding to benefit ourselves.

The Master summarized his teaching in the saying that understanding the Truth would set us free. This isn't an announcement of something we need to do, or something that must be done for us, to achieve our freedom, nor is it a statement about something in the future. Truth is what exists. He didn't say we must wait until something becomes true that isn't true right now. He said: "Understand what Truth is now, and you will discover that the Truth about yourself is Liberty." If understanding Truth sets us free, it can only be because we are already free in truth, we just don't realize it.

Our freedom lies in recreating within ourselves the same creative power of Thought that originally brought the world into being, "so that the things which are seen were not made of things which do appear." Therefore, let us boldly claim our inheritance as "sons and daughters of the Almighty," and by consistently thinking thoughts of goodness, beauty, and truth, create around ourselves circumstances that match our thinking, while through our guidance and example helping others to achieve the same.

XI: Yourself

I want to discuss the vitality that comes from being yourself. This approach has the advantage of being straightforward, since it must certainly be simpler to be yourself than to pretend to be someone or something else. However, this is exactly what countless people are constantly attempting to do; they find their authentic self inadequate, so they're perpetually trying to improve upon what God created them to be, resulting in endless tension and struggle. Naturally, they're correct to set before themselves an ideal far greater than anything they've achieved so far—the only way to make progress is by pursuing an ideal that stays one step ahead of us—but their error lies in failing to recognize that reaching this ideal requires growth, and growth must involve expanding something that already exists within us, which means accepting who we are and where we currently stand as our foundation. This development is an ongoing process, and we cannot accomplish next month's growth without first completing this month's; yet we consistently want to leap into some future ideal, failing to see that we can only reach it by steadily advancing from our present position.

These thoughts should give us greater confidence and comfort. We're using a power that's much stronger than we think we are, but it isn't separate from us and doesn't need to be convinced, forced, or tricked into doing what we want. This power is the foundation of our very existence, constantly rising up to show itself in the physical world and becoming the personal self that we often focus on without thinking about where it comes from. In reality, our outer self is just the surface expression of that deeper identity hidden far below in the depths, which is nothing less than the Spirit-of-Life that forms the basis of all manifestation.

Try to understand what this Spirit must be in its true nature— that is, separate from any conditions that come from the different relationships that naturally form between its various individual expressions. In its pure, unified state, what else could it be but pure life—the Essence of Life, if you prefer to call it that? Then understand that as the Essence of Life, it exists at the very core of each of its forms of expression with the same perfect simplicity that we can imagine in our most abstract ideas. From this perspective, we see it as the eternally self-creating power that flows into form to express itself.

This universal Essence-of-Life continuously transforms into form, and because we are part of Nature, we don't need to look beyond ourselves to discover the life-giving energy working with all its power. Therefore, all we need to do is let it emerge to the surface. We don't have to force it to rise any more than an engineer who drills a bore-pipe for an artesian well has to force the water to rise in it; the water does this through its own energy, shooting up like a fountain a hundred feet into the air. In the same way, we will discover a fountain of Essence-of-Life ready to spring up within ourselves, endless and constantly growing in its flow, as One taught long ago to a woman at a roadside well.

This emergence of Life-Essence doesn't belong to someone else—it belongs to us. We don't need extensive education, difficult work, or exhausting travels to reach it; it isn't controlled by any particular teacher or author whose classes we must take or whose books we must study to obtain it. It exists at our very core, and a bit of logical thinking about how anything becomes what it is will quickly show us that this vast, unlimited life must be the foundation and essence of who we are, flowing through every part of our existence.

Surely being this vast infinitude of living power must be enough to satisfy all our desires, and yet this wonderful ideal is nothing other than what we already are in principle—it is all there within ourselves now, only waiting for our recognition for its manifestation. It is not the Essence-of-Life that needs to grow, for that is eternally perfect in itself; but it is our recognition of it that needs to grow, and this growth cannot be forced. It must come through a natural process, the first requirement of which is to refrain from all straining after being something which at the present time we cannot naturally be. The Law of our Evolution has given us certain powers and opportunities, and our further development depends on our doing exactly what these powers and opportunities make it possible for us to do, here and now.

If we do what we're capable of doing today, it will create opportunities for us to accomplish something better tomorrow, and this way the growth process will continue in a healthy and joyful manner with rapidly increasing momentum. This approach is much easier than struggling to force things to become what they're not, and it also produces far more beneficial outcomes. This doesn't mean sitting idle and doing nothing, and there's plenty of opportunity to use all our mental abilities, but these abilities themselves emerge from the Essence-of-Life, and they're not the creative force itself, but rather what gives it direction. Now it's this driving force behind our various abilities that represents our true innermost self; and if we recognize the connection between what's innermost and what's outermost, we'll understand that we already possess everything we need for our unlimited growth in the future.

Our vitality simply comes from being ourselves, but more fully than before; when we understand this, we free ourselves from a heavy load of needless tension and struggle, and instead of the old turmoil and stress, we discover a joyful energy that knows it always possesses the necessary strength to express itself through forms of goodness and beauty. Does it really matter where this path takes us? When we follow the way of beauty and goodness, we will create beauty and goodness, bringing more joy into the world, regardless of what specific shape that joy might take.

We hold ourselves back when we try to determine exactly what kind of good we will create before we even begin. Instead of focusing on having or making something specific, we should concentrate on expressing everything we truly are. This expression will emerge naturally as we recognize the treasures we already possess and appreciate the beauty and positive aspects of who we are right now, setting aside the negative thoughts and criticisms that hide this goodness from our view. When we take this approach, we will be amazed to discover what potential exists within us as we are today, even in our current circumstances that we might consider unappealing. By starting to work immediately with whatever positive elements we can find and shifting our attention away from the negative aspects we have focused on before, the correct path will reveal itself to us, guiding us in remarkable ways toward developing abilities we never knew we had and experiencing joy we never imagined possible.

We have never strayed from our correct path; we've simply been walking backward on it instead of moving forward. Now that we've started following the path in the proper direction, we discover it's nothing other than the way of peace, the path of joy, and the road to eternal life. We can achieve these things by simply living naturally with ourselves. It's because we're trying to be or do something that isn't natural to us that we experience exhaustion and struggle, when we should find all our activities joyfully focused on goals that accomplish themselves through the power of the love we have for them. But when we make the great discovery of how to live naturally, we'll find it to be everything, and more than everything, we had ever wanted, and our daily life will become a constant joy to ourselves, and we'll radiate light and life wherever we go.

XII: Religious Opinions

The renowned and insightful author George Eliot shared her mature perspective on religious beliefs with these words: "I have too deep a belief in the power that exists in all genuine faith, and the spiritual decay that comes with having no faith, to have any desire left in me to argue against religion." This hadn't always been her position, because in her younger years she had possessed considerable inclination to argue against religious beliefs; however, the wisdom gained through a lifetime of experience brought her to this understanding of the importance of sincere faith, regardless of the specific beliefs or reasoning that might lead someone to it.

Tennyson reached the same conclusion and offers a gentle warning:

"O you who after toil and storm
You might seem to have reached a purer air,
Whose faith has been focused in all places,
Nor does it care to attach itself to any particular shape.
Leave your sister alone when she prays
Her early paradise, her joyful perspectives,
Nor should you confuse with shadowy hints

"A life that leads melodious days."

And so these two brilliant thinkers have given us a valuable lesson in wisdom that we would be wise to learn from. Let's examine how this applies specifically to our own situation.

The genuine expression of Higher Thought doesn't include any "negative propaganda." It consistently supports the Affirmative approach, and its main goal is to eliminate the destructive force that eats away at the foundation of any life that tries to focus on the Negative. Its aim is to build up rather than tear down. However, we frequently encounter people who have completely wrong ideas about what this movement is and what it's trying to accomplish, which not only prevents them from looking into it themselves but also stops others from doing the same. Sometimes this happens because the subject has been explained to them poorly—in a way that unnecessarily conflicts with the specific type of religious beliefs they're used to; but more often it occurs because they jump to conclusions about the whole thing, deciding that the movement goes against their religious views without bothering to find out what its principles actually are. In both situations, a few comments about how New Thought relates to existing forms of religious belief might be helpful.

The first thing to consider in any endeavor is: What goal are we trying to achieve? The objective determines what methods we should use, and if we keep the nature of that objective clearly in mind, then we won't introduce pointless complications into our approach. All of this seems too obvious to mention, but it's precisely the failure to understand this simple truth that has created the entire body of theological hatred, along with all the persecutions, massacres, and martyrdoms that stain the pages of history, turning so many of them into records of nothing but brutality and ignorance. Let us hope for a better record in the future; and if we're going to achieve it, it will be through adopting the simple principle stated here.

In our own country alone, the different types of churches and religious groups form an extensive list, but each one shares the same goal—to help individuals establish a meaningful relationship with the Divine Power. The simple fact that someone practices any religion at all shows they acknowledge God as the Source of life and everything that makes life possible. Therefore, the aim in every situation is to receive greater amounts of life, whether in this world or the next, from the Only Source where it can truly be found, and thus to build the kind of relationship with this Source that allows the believer to receive from It all the life they desire. This means that before anyone can consciously receive anything at all, they must first have confidence that such a relationship has actually been created. This kind of confidence is precisely what we mean by Faith.

The position of someone who lacks this confidence is either that no such Source exists, or that they have no way to access It; in either case, they feel left to fight alone against the entire universe without awareness of any Superior Power supporting them. They are thrown completely upon their own resources, unaware of the inner spring from which these resources can be continuously renewed. They are like a plant severed at the stem and placed in the ground without any roots, and as a result, that spiritual decay which George Eliot describes spreads over them, creating weakness, confusion, and fear, along with all their harmful effects, where there should be that strength, order, and confidence which form the very foundation of all progress toward any goal, whether personal success or service to others.

From the perspective of those who understand the principles of spiritual existence, such a person is disconnected from the source of their own Being. Beyond and deep within that external self that each of us recognizes as the thinking person operating through the physical brain as a tool, we possess roots that extend deeply into that Infinite which, in our normal conscious state, we perceive only faintly; and it is through this foundation of our own identity, reaching far down into the concealed depths of Being, that we extract from the invisible that continuous flow of Life which later, through our mental power, we transform into all those external manifestations that we require. Therefore, there exists a constant need for everyone to understand the profound truth that their entire identity is grounded in such a foundation, and that the soil in which this foundation is planted is that Universal Being which has no name except that of the One all-encompassing I AM.

The most important thing for each of us is to understand this basic truth about who we are, because we only truly live to the extent that we grasp this reality; therefore, anything that helps us reach this understanding should be carefully protected. When any form of religion helps a particular person achieve this goal, it becomes true religion for that individual. It might be incomplete, but it's genuine as far as it extends; and what's needed isn't to tear down someone's faith just because it's limited, but to broaden it. This expansion will come from the person themselves, since it's an internal development rather than something built from the outside.

Our approach to other people's religious beliefs shouldn't be like that of iconoclasts who ruthlessly tear down what we see as merely traditional idols (using Bacon's definition of the term). Instead, we should take the opposite approach by focusing on the positive and affirming elements we find in another person's faith, then gradually helping them understand what makes these elements affirming. Once they grasp the key to the strength that exists within their familiar form of belief, they'll naturally begin to see the contrast between that strength and the non-essential additions that have accumulated over time, which will gradually bring them into a broader and more liberated understanding. When someone goes through this kind of process, their thoughts will never be directed toward anything that suggests cutting themselves off from their spiritual foundation. Rather, they'll discover that the rooting and grounding in the Divine that they initially trusted was indeed genuine, but in a way that's far richer, more magnificent, and more expansive than their early, childlike understanding of it.

The question isn't how well someone else's religious beliefs can withstand ruthless logical examination, but rather how effectively those beliefs help them recognize their connection with Divine Spirit. This living demonstration proves the personal value of their beliefs, and no shift in their thinking can be beneficial unless it leads to a deeper awareness of Divine Spirit's vitality within them. For any change in perspective to represent genuine progress, it must emerge from our growing understanding of the true essence of the life that has already unfolded within us. When we comprehend why we are who we are at this moment, we can then look forward and perceive what this same life principle that has carried us to our current position is capable of achieving in the days ahead. We might not be able to see very far into the future, but we will understand where to take our next step, and that knowledge is enough to keep us moving forward.

What we need to do, then, is help others grow from the foundation they're already living by, rather than uprooting them and leaving them to die. We shouldn't be afraid of becoming all things to all people by focusing on the positive elements in each person's beliefs as our starting point, because what affirms and gives life is always true, and Truth is always unified and consistent with itself. Therefore, we never need to worry about being inconsistent as long as we stick to this approach. It's completely pointless to waste time analyzing the negative additions to other people's beliefs. When we do this, we risk pulling up the good along with the bad, and we'll definitely end up rubbing people the wrong way. Furthermore, by looking exclusively for the life-giving and positive elements, we'll benefit ourselves as well. We'll not only maintain our composure, but we'll often discover significant reserves of positive power where we initially saw nothing but worthless accumulations. In this way, we'll gain both in breadth of understanding and in valuable resources.

Of course, we must remain absolutely firm when it comes to the core of Truth—this must never be compromised—but as representatives of the New Thought, even in the smallest capacity, we should strive to demonstrate to others not that their religion is incorrect, but that whatever life-giving elements they discover within it are indeed life-giving because they form part of the One Truth, which remains constant regardless of how it is expressed. Just as half a loaf is preferable to having no bread at all, uninformed worship is better than no worship whatsoever, and uninformed faith surpasses having no faith. Our purpose is not to tear down this faith and worship, but rather to guide them toward greater understanding and clarity.

For this reason, we can assure anyone who asks that giving up their traditional form of worship is not required by New Thought; instead, the principles of this movement, when properly understood, will reveal far more meaning in that worship than they have ever recognized before. Truth is one; and once the truth that lies beneath the outward form is clearly grasped, keeping or abandoning that form will turn out to be a matter of personal preference regarding what form, or lack of form, best helps the individual person realize the Truth itself.

XIII: A Lesson from Browning

Perhaps you're familiar with a short poem by Browning titled "An Epistle Containing the Strange Medical Experiences of Karshish, the Arab Physician." The somewhat unusual concept involves an Arab physician traveling through Palestine shortly after the events described in the Gospel come to an end, who encounters Lazarus—the man Jesus brought back from the dead—and in a letter to a medical colleague describes the remarkable impact that his glimpse of the afterlife has had on the man who was restored to life. The poem deserves to be examined in its entirety; however, for now a few selected lines from various parts will have to serve to show the nature of the transformation that has occurred in Lazarus. After likening him to a beggar who, having suddenly come into unlimited riches, cannot manage to use them according to his needs, Karshish goes on to say:—

> "So here—we call the treasure knowledge, let's say,
> Expanded beyond physical capability—
> Heaven opened to a soul while still on earth,
> Earth imposed upon a soul's purpose while glimpsing heaven:
> The man is unaware of the magnitude, the total,
>
> "The value in proportion of all things."

In reality, he has become almost entirely aware of "The spiritual life around the earthly life:" The law of that is known to him as this, "His heart and mind are there, while his feet remain here," and the result is a complete loss of mental balance that makes him entirely unsuitable for handling the matters of everyday life.

Now there's no question that Browning had a much more serious purpose in writing this poem than simply recording a wild idea that crossed his mind. If we look beneath the surface, the overall tone of his writings makes it clear that, however he came by it, Browning possessed a profound understanding of the inner realm of spiritual forces that give birth to everything we observe in the outer world of physical manifestation. His works constantly reference the life that exists beyond the veil, and it's this hint of some hidden mystery beneath his words that has inspired the numerous efforts to understand his meaning through Browning Societies and similar groups—efforts that fail or succeed depending on whether they approach from "the outside" or from "the inside." No one was better equipped than the poet to recognize the tremendous benefits of inner knowledge, and for the same reason he's also equipped to caution us about the dangers encountered on the path to gaining it; for nowhere is it more accurate that

"A little knowledge is a dangerous thing,"

and this poem highlights one of the most significant of these dangers.

Through the character of Lazarus, he portrays a person who has genuinely understood the reality of the inner nature of existence, someone for whom the veil has been lifted, and who recognizes that the external and visible world originates from the internal and spiritual realm. However, this description depicts someone whose eyes have been so overwhelmed by the light that he has lost the ability to adjust his sight to the physical world. He now makes the same mistake from the perspective of "the inner" that he previously made from the perspective of "the outer," the mistake of assuming that there is no essential reality in the dimension of existence that his mind is not directly focused on. This represents a lack of mental equilibrium, whether it manifests by denying reality to the inner world or the outer world. To become so engrossed in theoretical concepts that one cannot put them into practical use in everyday life is to let our most profound thoughts dissolve into mere fantasies.

There is a world of philosophy in the simple statement that there can be no inside without an outside, and no outside without an inside; and the great secret in life lies in learning to see things in their completeness, and to understand the inside and the outside at the same time. Each of them without the other is merely an abstract concept, having no real existence, which we consider separately only for the purpose of examining the logical steps by which they are connected together as cause and effect. Nature does not separate them, for they cannot be separated; and the law of nature is the law of life. It is said of Pythagoras that, after he had led his students to the highest peaks of inner knowledge, he never failed to emphasize the opposite lesson of tracing out the steps by which these inner principles transform themselves into the familiar conditions of the outward things that surround us. The process of analysis is simply a method for discovering what springs in the realm of causes we need to touch in order to produce certain effects in the realm of manifestation. But this is not enough. We must also learn to calculate how those particular effects, when produced, will relate to the world of already existing effects among which we intend to introduce them, how they will modify these and be modified by these in return; and this calculation of effects is as necessary as the knowledge of causes.

We cannot emphasize too strongly that reality encompasses both an inner and outer dimension, a creative force and its resulting manifestation, and that anything less than complete wholeness represents an illusion on either side. Nothing could have been more distant from Browning's purpose than to discourage truth-seekers from exploring the fundamental principles of existence, since without understanding these principles, truth must forever remain shrouded in mystery; however, the lesson he seeks to teach us involves carefully maintaining the mental balance that alone allows us to cultivate those unlimited powers whose endless development represents the fullness of life. Above all, we must remember that love forms the essence of life, and that love expresses itself through service, while service springs from empathy, which is the ability to perceive situations from the perspective of those we wish to assist, while simultaneously understanding them within their proper context; therefore, if we hope to experience that love which serves as the deepest life-giving force even within our most profound inner capacities, we must keep it vibrant by preserving our connection to external life as being just as real as the inner principles it reflects.

XIV: The Spirit of Opulence

It's a significant error to think that we need to limit and deprive ourselves to develop greater power or effectiveness. This creates an understanding of Divine Power as so restricted that the best way we can use it is through a strategy of self-deprivation, whether physical or mental. Naturally, if we believe that some form of self-deprivation is essential for producing good work, then as long as we hold this belief, it actually becomes true for us. "Whatsoever is not of faith"—meaning, not aligned with our genuine belief—"is sin"; and by acting against what we truly believe, we introduce a sense of resistance to the Divine Spirit, which must inevitably weaken our efforts and surround us with a dark atmosphere of doubt and lack of joy.

But all of this exists within our beliefs and is created by them; when we examine the foundation of these beliefs, we discover they're based on a complete misunderstanding of our own power's true nature. If we truly understand that our creative ability is limitless, then there's no reason to restrict how much we can enjoy what we create through this power. When we're drawing from something infinite, we never need to worry about taking more than we deserve. That's not where the real danger lies. The real danger comes from not fully recognizing our own abundance, and from mistaking the external results of our creative power for true wealth instead of recognizing that the creative power of spirit itself is the real treasure.

If we steer clear of this mistake, we don't need to restrict ourselves when drawing from the endless treasure trove: "All things are yours." The way to prevent this mistake is by understanding that genuine wealth lies in aligning ourselves with the spirit of abundance. We need to embrace abundance in our thinking. Don't focus specifically on "thinking money," since it's merely one form of abundance; instead, think abundance—think expansively, generously, and freely—and you'll discover that the ways to make this thinking real will come to you from every direction, whether as money or as countless other valuable things that can't be measured in dollars.

We shouldn't make ourselves dependent on any specific type of wealth, or demand that it comes to us through one particular path—doing so immediately creates limitations and blocks other forms of wealth while closing off alternative channels. Instead, we need to embrace the essence of wealth itself. This essence is Life, and throughout the universe, Life fundamentally operates through circulation, whether within an individual's physical body or across the vast scale of an entire solar system. Circulation involves a continuous flow in all directions, and the spirit of abundance follows this same universal principle that governs all life.

When this principle becomes clear to us, we'll see that our attention should focus more on giving than on receiving. We must view ourselves not as misers' treasure chests to be kept locked for our own benefit, but as centers of distribution; and the better we fulfill our function as such centers, the greater the corresponding inflow will be. If we block the outlet, the current must slow down, and a full and free flow can only be achieved by keeping it open. The spirit of abundance—the abundant way of thinking, that is— consists of cultivating the feeling that we possess all kinds of riches which we can give to others, and which we can give generously because through this very action we open the way for even greater supplies to flow in. But you say, "I don't have enough money, I barely know how to pay for necessities. What do I have to give?"

The answer is that we must always begin from where we currently stand; and if your wealth right now isn't plentiful on the material level, you don't need to worry about starting there. There are other kinds of wealth, even more precious, on the spiritual and intellectual levels, which you can offer; and you can begin from this position and cultivate the mindset of abundance, even if your bank account balance might be zero. And then the universal law of attraction will start to take effect. You will not only begin to feel an influx on the spiritual and intellectual levels, but this will spread to the material level as well.

If you have truly grasped the essence of abundance, you will naturally attract material prosperity as well as the deeper forms of wealth that cannot be measured in monetary terms. Because you genuinely comprehend the nature of abundance, you will neither pretend to look down upon material wealth nor will you assign it importance it doesn't deserve. Instead, you will harmonize it with your other, more inner forms of riches so that it serves as a practical tool for facilitating their fuller expression. When used in this way, with a clear understanding of how it relates to spiritual and intellectual wealth, material prosperity becomes unified with them, and should neither be avoided and feared nor pursued for its own sake.

Money itself isn't evil—it's the obsession with money that creates problems. A mindset of abundance is actually the complete opposite of being greedy for money's sake. This mindset doesn't worship money. Instead, it embraces a generous spirit that naturally understands the fundamental principle of giving and receiving. When approaching any project or opportunity, this mindset doesn't first ask, "What's in it for me?" but rather, "What can I contribute?" When we make contribution our primary focus, the rewards flow back to us abundantly, naturally, and in exactly the right ways—something that never happens when our main concern is only what we can get.

We aren't expected to give what we don't yet possess or to go into debt; instead, we should give generously from what we already have, understanding that by doing this we activate the law of circulation, and as this law brings us increasingly greater flows of all kinds of good things, our giving will also grow, not by denying ourselves any growth in our own lives that we might want, but by discovering that every expansion makes us more powerful tools for expanding the lives of others. "Live and let live" is the motto of true abundance.

XV: Beauty

Do we focus our thoughts enough on the subject of Beauty? I don't think we do. We tend to view Beauty as something merely surface-level and fail to understand everything it represents. This wasn't true for the great thinkers of the ancient world—look at the position that someone as significant as Plato assigned to Beauty as the expression of everything highest and greatest in the universe's system. These great minds of antiquity weren't shallow thinkers, and therefore would never have placed something that is only superficial in the supreme position. So we would be wise to ask what these brilliant minds discovered in the concept of Beauty that made it appeal to them as the most perfect outward expression of everything that lies deepest in the fundamental laws of Being. It's because, when properly understood, Beauty represents the highest living quality of Thought. It's the magnificent overflowing abundance of Love that signals the presence of infinite reserves of Power supporting it. It's the joyful abundance that demonstrates the possession of inexhaustible stores of wealth that can afford to be so generous while remaining just as limitless as before. When interpreted correctly, Beauty serves as the indicator of the entire nature of Being.

Beauty is the outward expression of Harmony, and Harmony is the coordinated functioning of all the forces of Being, both within the individual and in the relationship between the individual and the Infinite from which it emerges; therefore this Harmony leads us directly into the presence of the innermost undifferentiated Life. In this way, Beauty maintains the most immediate connection with the very mystery of Life; it is the radiant glory that spreads itself across the sanctuary of the Divine Spirit. When we look at it from the outside, Beauty belongs to the artist and the poet, and it captures our emotions and speaks directly to the deepest feelings of our heart, awakening the response of that part within us which recognizes itself in the harmony we perceive externally, but this happens only because it crosses the bridge of Reason with such swift movement that we travel from the outermost to the innermost and back again in an instant; yet the bridge remains there and, if we retrace our steps more slowly, we will discover that, when viewed from within, Beauty is equally the domain of the calm reasoner and analyst.

What the poet and the artist grasp through intuition, the analyst develops step by step, but the outcome is identical in both situations; for no intuition is genuine unless it can be expanded into a rational sequence of understandable elements, and no argument is valid unless it can be compressed into that swift insight which is intuition.

Both the passionate artist and the thoughtful philosopher discover that genuine Beauty emerges naturally from the actual structure of what it represents. Beauty isn't something tacked on as an afterthought, but rather something that already exists within the original concept, something that the idea naturally develops toward, and which requires that foundational idea to give it any reason for being. The measure of Beauty lies in this question: What does it express? Is it merely a surface treatment, a layer of paint applied from the outside? If so, it's nothing more than a whitewashed tomb, a facade meant to conceal the emptiness or ugliness that should be eliminated. But does it arise as the genuine and natural result of what lies beneath the surface? Then it serves as evidence of abundant Life and Love and Intelligence, which refuses to settle for mere practicality that rushes to escape the work of creation as quickly as possible, as if fleeing from a forced and unwanted duty. Instead, it delights in its work and remains reluctant to abandon it until it has expressed this joy through every perfect detail of form and color and beautiful proportion that the material allows, all while never straying even slightly from the original intent of the design.

Wherever we discover Beauty, we can deduce that an immense reservoir of Power lies behind it; indeed, we can view it as the visible manifestation of the profound truth that Life-Power is limitless. When the deeper significance of Beauty becomes clear to us in this way, and we come to understand it as the complete abundance and overflow of Power, we will discover that we have acquired a fresh standard to guide our own lives. We need to start applying this remarkable process that we have learned from Nature. Having discovered how Nature operates—how God operates—we must begin to function in the same way, and never regard any work as finished until we have brought it to some final expression of Beauty, whether physical, intellectual, or spiritual. Is my purpose good? That represents the fundamental question, because the purpose determines the character of the essence in all things. What is the most beautiful way in which I can express the good I aim for? That represents the final question; because the genuine Beauty that our work displays measures the Power, Intelligence, Love—in other words, the amount and quality of our own life that we have invested in it. Genuine Beauty, understand—that which is beautiful because it most completely expresses the original concept, not mere decoration that occupies our minds as something separate from the intended purpose.

Nothing is so insignificant that it doesn't possess its complete power of expression through some form of Beauty that is uniquely its own. Beauty represents the law of perfect Thought, whether our Thought concerns a plan affecting millions of people or a word spoken to a small child. True Beauty and true Power are interconnected with each other. Kind expression comes from kind thought, and kind expression forms the essence of Beauty, which, in seeking to express itself with ever greater perfection, becomes that refined touch of sympathy that constitutes artistic skill, whether applied to working with physical materials or with human emotions. But remember, first comes Use, then Beauty, and neither is complete without the other. Use without Beauty represents graceless giving, and Beauty without Use is pretense; never forget, however, that there exists a realm of the mind where the use is discovered in the beauty, where Beauty itself serves the direct purpose of lifting us to perceive a higher ideal that will from then on flow through our lives, bringing a more vibrant quality to everything we think and say and do.

When viewed this way, the Beautiful represents the genuine expression of the Good. No matter which perspective we take, we'll discover that they precisely correspond to each other. They are essentially the same thing, manifesting in the external and internal realms respectively. However, as we seek a higher Beauty than what we've previously discovered, we must be careful not to overlook the Beauty that already exists around us. Perfect harmony with one's surroundings, combined with perfect expression of one's inner nature, is what creates Beauty; our lack of understanding about the nature of something or its environment might blind us to the Beauty it already possesses. It requires the genius of a Millet with paint, or a Whitman with words, to reveal the beauty in those ordinary, everyday people who make up most of our world, whose real-life counterparts we walk past as if they possess no form or attractiveness. Certainly, the mission of every thoughtful man and woman is to help create forms of greater beauty—spiritual, intellectual, and material—in all areas; but if we want to create something more magnificent than Watteau gardens or Dresden china shepherdesses, we must join the great realistic school of Nature and learn to recognize the beauty that already exists around us, even when it might have some dirt on the surface. Then, once we've learned the fundamental principles of Beauty from the All-Spirit which embodies it, we'll understand how to develop Beauty along its natural path without preserving the dirt; and we'll realize that all Beauty expresses Living Power, and that we can measure our power by how much beauty we can transform it into, making our lives,

"Through the beauty of flawless actions,"
"More powerful than any poetic imagination."

———————

XVI: Separation and Unity

Chapter 1

"The prince of this world cometh, and hath nothing in Me" (John xiv, 30). In these words, the Grand Master of Divine Science provides us with the key to the Great Knowledge. When we compare this with other passages, we see that the terms translated here as "prince" and "world" could just as easily be translated as "principle" and "age." Jesus is speaking here about a principle of the present age that stands in complete opposition to the principle he himself visibly represented, having no place within him whatsoever. This principle represents the complete contradiction of everything Jesus came to teach and demonstrate. Jesus described his own mission as coming "to bear witness to the Truth," and so that people "might have life, and that they might have it more abundantly." Therefore, the principle he refers to must be the exact opposite of Truth and Life—meaning it must be the principle of Falsehood and Death.

What, then, is this false and destructive principle that governs our current era? When we examine the essence of the entire discussion that these words conclude, we discover that the central concept Jesus had been working most earnestly to instill in his disciples during their final gathering before the crucifixion was the absolute identity and complete oneness of "the Father" and "the Son"—the principle of perfect unity between God and humanity. If this was the great Truth he was so urgently concerned with impressing upon his disciples' minds when his physical presence would soon be taken from them—the Truth of Unity—can we not reasonably conclude that the opposing falsehood is the claim of separation, the assertion that God and humanity are not one? The concept of separation is exactly the principle upon which the world has operated from that day until now—the assumption that God and humanity are not unified in being, and that matter possesses a different essence from spirit. In other words, the principle that appeals to the intellectual thinking of our present age is that of duality—the notion of two powers and two substances that are opposite in nature and therefore hostile to each other, pervading all things and consequently leaving no completeness anywhere.

The entire purpose of the Bible is to challenge the concept of two opposing forces existing in the world. The good news is described as one of "reconciliation" (2 Cor. v. 18), where we are also informed that "all things are from God," therefore leaving no space for any other power or any other substance; and the great deception, which the Good News aims to reveal, is proclaimed throughout the Bible to be the suggestion of duality, which represents some alternative mode of Life that is not the One Life, but something distinct from it—a concept that cannot be clearly articulated without creating a logical contradiction. Throughout the Bible, the fiction of the duality of separation is exposed as the great deception, but nowhere in such a forceful and focused way as in that remarkable passage in Revelations where it is represented through the mysterious Number of the Beast. "He that hath understanding let him count the number of the Beast ... and his number is six hundred and sixty and six" (Rev. xiii, 18, R.V.). Allow me to highlight the great principle conveyed in this mysterious number. It has other more specific applications, but this one fundamental principle forms the foundation of them all.

It is a well-established principle that every unity contains within itself a trinity, just as each individual person consists of body, soul, and spirit. If we want to fully understand anything, we must be able to grasp it in its threefold nature; therefore in symbolic numbering, multiplying the unit by three suggests the completeness of what that unit represents; and similarly, repeating a number three times represents its extension to infinity. Now observe what happens when we apply these representative methods of numerical expression to the principles of Oneness and separateness respectively. Oneness is Unity, and $1 \times 3 = 3$, which, when intensified to its highest expression, is written as 333. Now apply the same method to the concept of separateness. Separateness consists of one and another one, each of which, according to the universal law, contains a trinity. In this understanding of duality, the totality of things is two, and $2 \times 3 = 6$, and when we intensify this to its highest expression, we get 666, which is the Number of the Beast.

Why of the Beast? Because being separate from God, or the duality of opposition, which is also a duality of polarity, which is Dual-Unity, recognizes something as having essential being, which is not the One Spirit; and such a concept can only be expressed in words by some term that in common understanding represents something, not only lower than the divine, but lower than the human as well. It is because the idea of oneself as a being separate from God, if followed through to its logical conclusions, must ultimately lead all who embrace it to a state of affairs where open savagery or hidden cunning, the tiger nature or the serpent nature, can be the only possible rule of action.

The principle that governs our current era cannot coexist with the principle of Perfect Wholeness that the Great Master demonstrated through His teachings and His very being. These two concepts are completely incompatible, and whichever one we choose as our guiding principle must completely exclude the other; we cannot serve both God and material wealth. There is no such thing as being partially whole. Either we remain trapped in the principle of Separateness, with our eyes still closed to the true nature of the Kingdom of Heaven; or we have understood the principle of Unity without any exceptions whatsoever, where the One Being encompasses everything—both body and soul, the visible form and the invisible essence and life of all things equally. Nothing can be excluded, and we stand complete in this very moment, missing no ability, needing only to become aware of our own capabilities and to learn to trust them by "having them strengthened through practice."

The following message from "A Foreign Reader," discussing the Number of the Beast as examined by Judge Troward in "Separation and Unity," comes from EXPRESSION for 1902, where it was originally published. What follows is Judge Troward's response to this letter.

Dear Mr. Editor—A correspondent in the current issue of Expression highlights the reference in the Book of Revelation to the number 666 as the mark of the Beast, since the trinity of mind, soul, and body, when viewed as a unified whole, can be represented by the number 333, and therefore duality equals 333 $\times$ 2 = 666.

I believe the reverse of this idea is even more remarkable, and I want to highlight it. Rather than multiplying, let's attempt division. First, take unity as the number one and divide it by three (which naturally represents the same formula: mind, soul, and body). When written as a common fraction, it's simply 1/3, which is an incomplete mathematical expression. However, if we use the decimal form of one divided by three, we get .3 repeating, meaning .3333 continuing forever. Put differently, when we apply mathematics to this proposition by dividing the formula of spirit, soul, and body into unity, it maintains its truth endlessly.

Now we come to consider it as a duality in the same way. When expressed as a common fraction it is 2/3; but as a decimal fraction it is .6666 continuing infinitely. I think this is worth noting.

Yours very faithfully,

A Foreign Reader.

Brussels, August 14, 1902.

Dear Editor,

I'm returning the very interesting letter that came with yours, and I want to thank you for sharing it. I'm delighted that my article helped bring out additional insights on this topic.

This also provides an excellent example of one fundamental principle of Unity, which is that Unity reproduces itself in each of its parts, so that every part taken individually is an exact reproduction (in principles) of the greater Unity of which it forms a portion. Therefore, if you take the individual person as your unit (which is what I did), and proceed through multiplication, you get the results that were pointed out in my article. And conversely, if you take the Great Unity of All-Being as your unit, and proceed through division, you arrive at the result shown by your foreign correspondent. The principle is purely mathematical, and is extremely interesting in the present application as it shows the existence of a system of hidden mathematics running throughout the entire Bible. This supports what I said in my article that there were other applications of the principle in question, though this particular one did not occur to me at the time.

I owe a great debt to your correspondent for providing additional evidence that confirms the accuracy of my interpretation of the Number of the Beast. Both of our interpretations reinforce one another, since they are simply different methods of expressing the same concept, and they possess this benefit over those commonly offered: they do not point to any specific type of evil, but instead articulate a universal principle that applies to all forms equally.

Yours sincerely,

T.

London, August 30, 1902.

Chapter 2

It might help clarify my point if I remind readers that the conflict between the principles of Unity and separation was what led to Jesus's crucifixion. We need to distinguish between the charge that actually caused his death and the purely technical charge on which the Roman Governor sentenced him. The latter—the charge of opposing Caesar's royal authority—has its importance; but it's evident from the biblical record that this was merely a formality, with the real reason for conviction being found in the statement of the chief priests: "We have a law, and by our law he ought to die, because he made himself the Son of God."

The conflict between the two principles of Unity and separation was first openly revealed when Jesus made his famous statement, "I and my Father are one." The Jews picked up stones to stone him. Jesus then said to them, "Many good works have I shown you from my Father; for which of those works do you stone me?" The Jews answered, "For a good work we stone you not; but for blasphemy; and because you, being a man, make yourself God." Jesus responded, "Is it not written in your law, I said you are gods? If He called them gods, to whom the Word of God came (and the Scriptures cannot be broken), do you say of him, whom the Father has sanctified, and sent into the world, you blaspheme; because I said, I am the Son of God?" Here we see the first open confrontation between the two opposing principles that eventually led to the scene at Calvary as Jesus's final testimony to the principle of Unity. He died because he upheld the Truth; that he was one with the Father. That was the essential charge for which he was executed. "Are you the son of the Blessed?" he was asked by the priestly court; and the answer came clear and definitive, "I am." Then the Council said, "He has spoken blasphemy, what further need do we have of witnesses?" And they all condemned him as deserving of death.

Jesus chose not to engage in a pointless debate with judges whose thinking was so deeply entrenched in dualistic concepts that they couldn't consider any alternative viewpoint; however, when addressing a diverse crowd that wasn't officially bound to any particular system, the situation was entirely different. Within this group, there might still be individuals who remained open to persuasion, so Jesus made his appeal by referencing a passage from the Psalms that everyone present knew well, highlighting how the very people to whom God's word was directed were called "gods" by the Divine Speaker Himself. He emphasized the undeniable nature of this fact by stressing that it came from "Scripture which cannot be broken," and he made the intended meaning of this statement clear through the argument he drew from it. Jesus essentially said, "You want to stone me as a blasphemer for claiming about myself what your own Scriptures declare about each one of you." He argued that his claim of unity with "the Father" wasn't something unique to him alone, but rather something that Scripture, when properly understood, gave every single person listening the right to claim for themselves.

Throughout his teachings, we consistently see that Jesus never makes a claim about himself that he doesn't also extend to those who embrace his message. When he tells the Jews, "You belong to this world; I do not belong to this world," he similarly says about his disciples, "They do not belong to the world, just as I do not belong to the world." When he declares, "I am the light of the world," he likewise tells them, "You are the light of the world." When he states, "I and my Father are one," he equally prays that they all might be one, just as we are one. When he is called "the Son of God," St. John writes, "To them he gave the power to become sons of God, to all who believe in his name;" and by believing in the name, we can certainly understand this as believing in the principle that the name represents in words.

The fundamental unity between God and humanity stands as the central truth that runs through everything Jesus taught. He presented himself as the living embodiment of this principle. He pointed to his miracles as evidence of this truth, saying "it is the Father that doeth the works." This concept formed the core of his final conversation with his disciples on the night of his betrayal. This is the Truth that he told Pilate was the very purpose of his existence—to bear witness to it. He died defending this Truth, and through the living power of this same Truth, he was resurrected. The entire purpose of his mission was to help people understand their unity with God and grasp the inevitable consequences that flow from this realization. He sought to lead them away from the dualistic thinking that creates an unbridgeable divide between God and humanity, making any genuine understanding of the Principle of Life impossible. Instead, he wanted to guide them toward a clear recognition of Life's deepest nature—that each person shares an inherent identity with that Infinite, all-encompassing Spirit of Life that he referred to as "the Father."

"The branch cannot bear fruit except it abide in the vine;" the ability to bear fruit, to create and to give forth, relies completely on the reality that each person is, and remains forever, as much an essential part of Universal Spirit as the fruit-bearing branch is an essential part of the main stem. Abandon this understanding, and view God as simply an outside Creator who might command us, or perhaps occasionally respond to our pleas and requests, and we have abandoned the foundation of Life itself along with any chance for growth or freedom. This represents dualism, which separates us from our Source of Life; and as long as we accept this mistaken idea as the true principle of Being, we will discover ourselves restricted by limitations and unsolvable problems of every kind: We have lost the Key of Life and therefore cannot open the door.

But to the extent that we remain in the vine—meaning we consciously recognize our constant unity with the Originating Spirit—and remind ourselves that this unity isn't given as a reward for good deeds or as a special favor (which would contradict the Unity itself, since any act of giving would immediately suggest separation), but instead focus on the truth that this unity is the deepest and most fundamental aspect of our own nature; to the extent that we consciously understand this, we will achieve greater and greater certainty in our knowledge, leading to increasingly perfect outward expression, whose growing brilliance has no boundaries; because it is the continuous flow of the inexhaustible Spirit of Life expressing itself through what we know as our individual existence.

The idea of dualism acts as a barrier that stops people from seeing this truth, causing them to stumble around blindly through endless confusion and complexity. However, as St. Paul correctly states, when this barrier is removed, we will discover ourselves transformed from glory to glory as by the Lord the Spirit. "His name shall be called Immanuel," which means "God in us," not a separate entity apart from ourselves. We should remember that Jesus was condemned by the principle of separation precisely because he represented the outward expression of the principle of Unity. By holding fast to the principle of Unity, we are clinging to the only possible foundation of Life and upholding the Truth for which Jesus gave his life.

XVII: Externalisation

Who wouldn't want to be happy with themselves and their situation? That's what we all want—a fuller life, greater and brighter energy within ourselves, and fewer limitations in our environment. We're told that the key to achieving this is through our thoughts. We're told to change how we think, and improved conditions will naturally follow. However, many people searching for answers feel this is like being told to catch birds by sprinkling salt on their tails. If we can manage to put salt on a bird's tail, we might as well just grab the bird with our hands. If we can truly change our thinking, then we can indeed transform our circumstances.

But how can we create this shift in cause that will then produce the changed outcome we want? This is the hands-on question that troubles many sincere seekers. They can understand clearly enough the entire chain of cause and effect that leads to manifesting their desired results, if only they could overcome that one initial obstacle. The challenge is genuine, and until it gets resolved, it undermines all the teaching and turns it into nothing but theory on paper. This is why students should focus their attention especially on this particular point. They sense the need for some firm foundation from which they can actually change their thinking, and until they discover this, the theory of Divine Science, no matter how complete it may be, will stay nothing more than mere theory for them, creating no real-world results.

The necessary scientific foundation exists, however, and is remarkably simple and logical, provided we take the effort to think it through carefully ourselves. Unless we are willing to defend the argument that the Power that created the universe is fundamentally evil, or that the universe is the product of two opposing and equal forces, one evil and the other good—both of which claims are provably false—we have no choice but to conclude that the Original Source of everything must be fundamentally good. It cannot be partially good and partially evil, because that would put it in conflict with itself and make it self-destructive; therefore it must be entirely good. But once we accept this basic premise, we eliminate the foundation of all evil. For how can evil emerge from an All-creating Source that is completely good, and in which, consequently, no seed for evil's development can be found? Good cannot be the source of evil; and since nothing can emerge except from the one Original Mind, which is purely good, the true essence of all things must be what they have inherited from their Source—namely, good.

Therefore, it follows that evil is not the fundamental nature of anything, and evil must originate from something outside the true nature of things. Since evil does not exist in the true nature of things themselves, nor in the Universal Mind which serves as the Originating Principle, only one source remains for it to emerge from, and that is our own individual thought. Initially, we assume that evil is as naturally inherent in things as good is—an assumption we would never make if we paused to consider the essential nature of the Originating Principle. Then, based on this completely unfounded assumption, we construct a framework of fears that naturally follow from this belief; in this way, we feed and give reality to the Negative, or that which has no real existence beyond what we assign to it, until we begin to view it as possessing its own Affirmative power, and thus establish a false concept of Being—created by our own minds—to challenge the rightful claims of true Being to rule over the universe.

Once we assume that two competing forces exist—one good and the other evil—controlling the universe, any sense of harmony becomes impossible; the entire natural order is disrupted, and whether for ourselves or for the world as a whole, no foundation of certainty remains anywhere. This is exactly the situation in which most people find themselves living. They exist surrounded by endless uncertainty about everything, and as a result become victims of constant fears and worries; the only way to escape from this condition is to address the fundamental issue and understand that the entire structure of evil stems from our own mistaken understanding of the nature of Being.

But once we understand that the true nature of Being inherently excludes any possibility of evil, we'll recognize that when we surrender to thoughts and fears about evil, we're giving reality to something that has no genuine substance, and we're granting the Negative a positive power it doesn't actually have—essentially, we're bringing into existence the very thing we're afraid of. The solution to this is to always return to the fundamental nature of Being as completely Good, and then tell ourselves: "My thoughts must constantly create external reality, because that's their essential nature, which can never be changed. So will I create God or God's opposite? What do I want to see expressed in my life—Good or its opposite? Will I bring forth what I know to be true reality or its reverse?" This leads to the unwavering decision to always express God, or Good, because that represents the only genuine reality in everything; and this decision carries power because it rests on the solid foundation of Truth.

We must refuse to acknowledge evil; we must refuse to accept that there is any such thing to be acknowledged. The opposite of this principle is what the story of the Fall represents. "In the day that you eat of it you shall surely die" was never said about knowing Good, because Good never brought death into the world. It is consuming the fruit from the tree of a supposed knowledge that includes a second aspect—the knowledge of evil—that becomes the source of death. Accept that evil has real substance, making it something that can be known, and you create it along with all its resulting consequences of suffering, illness and death. But "be certain that the Lord He is God"—meaning that the one and Only Governing Principle of the universe, whether inside us or surrounding us, is Good and Good alone—and evil with all its accompanying effects returns to its original state of nothingness, and we discover that the Truth has set us free. We are free to manifest whatever we choose, whether within ourselves or in our circumstances, because we have discovered the firm foundation on which to make the necessary shift in mental perspective through the fact that Good is the only true reality of Being.

1902.

XVIII: Entering into the Spirit of It

"Entering into the spirit of it." What a familiar phrase! Yet how much it truly encompasses, how absolutely everything! We immerse ourselves in the spirit of a project, in the spirit of a cause, in the spirit of a writer, even in the spirit of a game; and this makes all the difference both for us and for whatever we engage with. A game lacking spirit becomes a dreary experience; an organization without spirit crumbles apart; and a project devoid of spirit is destined to fail. Conversely, the book that seems meaningless to an unsympathetic reader overflows with vitality and insight for someone who connects with the author's spirit; the person who embraces the spirit of music discovers a wellspring of renewal in an excellent performance that completely escapes the detached critic who attends merely to evaluate by inflexible standards; and this pattern holds true in every situation we can imagine. When we fail to connect with the spirit of something, it provides no energizing influence on us, and we perceive it as boring, bland, and without value. This reflects our daily reality, and these are the terms we use to describe it. The language is perfectly chosen. It reveals our instinctive understanding of spirit as the essential truth in everything, regardless of its size or significance. When we align ourselves properly with the spirit of something, everything else will naturally fall into place.

By immersing ourselves in the essence of anything, we create a mutual exchange of energy between it and ourselves. We breathe life into it through our own vitality, while it energizes us with a vibrant interest that we recognize as its essence. Therefore, the more deeply we connect with the essence of everything we encounter, the more fully alive we become. The more completely we achieve this connection, the more we discover that we are uncovering the fundamental secret of Life. While it might sound obvious, the great secret of Life lies in its very aliveness, and it is precisely more of this quality of aliveness that we seek to embrace. This is the precious gift we can never possess in excess.

But every fact also contains its opposite, and we can never truly understand something until we know not only what it is, but also clearly grasp what it is not. For complete understanding, knowing the negative is just as essential as knowing the positive; perfect knowledge comes from recognizing the relationship between these two aspects, and perfect power develops from this knowledge by allowing us to balance the positive and negative against each other in whatever proportion we choose, bringing flexibility to what would otherwise be too rigid, and giving structure to what would otherwise be too fluid; and so, by combining these two extremes, we can create any outcome we desire. This reflects the ancient Hermetic principle, "Coagula et solve"—"Solidify the fluid and dissolve the solid"; therefore, if we want to discover the secret of "entering into the spirit of it," we must understand something about the negative, which represents the "not-spirit."

In different eras this negative phase has been expressed through various forms of language suited to the spirit of those times; and so, dressing this concept in the clothing of today, I will summarize the opposite of Spirit with the word "Mechanism." Above all else this is a mechanical age, and it is remarkable how much of what we call our social progress has its foundation in the mechanical arts. Strip away the mechanical arts to what they were during the time of the Plantagenets and most of our celebrated civilization would retreat back through the centuries alongside them. We might not be aware of all this, but the mechanical tendency of our era has a strong hold on society as a whole. We routinely examine the mechanical aspect of things rather than any other perspective. Everything is accomplished mechanically, from the carving on a piece of furniture to the organization of the social system. It is the mechanism that must be examined first, and the spirit must be made to fit the mechanical requirements. We step into the mechanism of it rather than into the Spirit of it, and thus we restrict the Spirit and refuse to allow it to follow its own path; and then, as a result, we achieve entirely mechanical action, and complete our cycle of ignorance by assuming that this is the only type of action that exists.

Yet this isn't necessarily how things must be, even when it comes to physical science. The scientists who have made the greatest breakthroughs are those who have most clearly understood that the mechanical is subordinate to the spiritual. A person who can only recognize a natural law when it operates through specific mechanical forms they're already familiar with will never advance to creating the more sophisticated mechanisms that could be built upon that law, because they fail to understand that it's the law that determines the mechanism, not the other way around. This person will make no progress in science, whether theoretical or practical, and the world will never be indebted to them. However, the person who understands that the mechanism for applying any principle emerges from truly comprehending the principle will study the principle first, knowing that once it's properly understood, it will naturally reveal everything needed to put it to practical use.

And if this holds true for what we call physical science, it's even more applicable to the Science of Spirit. There's a mechanical way of thinking that evaluates everything based on the constraints of past experiences, failing to account for the fact that those experiences were largely the products of our lack of understanding about spiritual law. However, when we grasp the true law of Being, we'll transcend these mechanical concepts. We won't reject the reality of the body or the physical world as actual things, understanding that they too are Spirit, but we'll learn to reject their power as causes. We'll learn to differentiate between the causa causta and the causa causans, the secondary or apparent physical cause and the primary or spiritual cause, without which the secondary cause couldn't exist; and in this way we'll gain a new perspective of clear knowledge and definite power by crossing the threshold of the mechanical and entering into its spirit.

What we need to do is maintain our balanced position between these two extremes, rejecting neither Spirit nor the mechanism that serves as its form and through which it operates. One is just as essential to a complete whole as the other, because there must be an exterior as well as an interior; we simply must remember that the creative principle always resides inside, and that the exterior only displays what the interior creates. Therefore, whatever external result we want to produce, we must first enter into the spirit of it and work with the spiritual principle, whether within ourselves or others; and by doing this our understanding will become greatly expanded, because from the outside we can see only one small section of the circumference, while from the center we can see all of it. If we completely understand the truth that Spirit is Creator, we can do away with difficult investigations into the mechanical aspect of all our problems. If we are building from the outside, then we have to calculate nervously the strength of our materials and the force of every push and pressure to which they might be exposed, and quite possibly after everything we may discover that we have made an error somewhere in our complex calculations. But if we recognize the power of creating from within, we shall discover all these calculations correctly done for us; because the same Spirit which is Creator is also what the Bible calls "the Wonderful Numberer." Building from the outside is based on analysis, and no analysis is complete without precise quantitative knowledge; but creation is the complete opposite of analysis, and brings its own mathematics along with it.

To truly understand the essence of anything, you must unite your thoughts with the creative force at its core; so why not go directly to the heart of everything and connect with the Spirit of Life itself? You might wonder where to find this spirit? It exists within you; and the more you discover it there, the more you'll recognize it everywhere around you. View Life as the one fundamental reality, whether it exists in you or surrounds you; try to grasp its living essence, and then seek to connect with its Spirit by declaring it to be the entirety of what you are. Keep affirming this truth in your thoughts, and gradually this affirmation will develop into a genuine living force within you, making it second nature, until you find it impossible and unnatural to think any other way; and the closer you come to this realization, the greater your mastery will become over both your body and your circumstances, until finally you will so completely enter into its Spirit—into the Spirit of the Divine creative power that forms the foundation of all existence—that, as Jesus said, "nothing shall be impossible to you," because you have so fully entered into its Spirit that you discover yourself to be one with it. Then all the old restrictions will have disappeared, and you will be living in a completely new world of Life, Liberty and Love, with yourself as the radiating center. You will understand the truth that your Thought is an unlimited creative power, and that you yourself stand behind your Thought, controlling and directing it with Knowledge for any purpose that Love inspires and Wisdom designs. In this way you will stop your labors, your struggles and worries, and enter into that new order where perfect rest combines with endless activity.

XIX: The Bible and the New Thought

Chapter 1: The Son

A fascinating topic for anyone studying the New Thought movement is examining how precisely its teachings align with biblical teachings. There isn't actually such a thing as new thought in terms of new Truth, because what is true today must have always been true; however, there is such a thing as a fresh presentation of ancient Truth, and this is where the novelty of the current movement lies. Yet this same Truth has been expressed repeatedly throughout earlier periods in different forms and with varying degrees of completeness, and nowhere more thoroughly than in the Scriptures of the Old and New Testaments. None of the earlier forms of expression is more widely recognized by our readers than what appears in the Bible, and no other is woven into our hearts with the same sacred and loving connections: therefore, I don't hesitate to say that the presence of a clear connection between its teaching and that of the New Thought must be a source of strength and encouragement to any of us who have been used to looking to the old and revered Book as a treasury of Divine wisdom in the past. We will discover that the brighter light will smooth the difficult passages and illuminate the unclear ones, and that regarding the treasures of knowledge concealed in the ancient text, we haven't been told even half of what exists.

The Bible places strong emphasis on "the glorious liberty of the sons of God," bringing together in one phrase the dual concept of childlike dependence and individual freedom. A thorough examination of this topic will reveal that these two concepts are not in conflict with each other, but rather are essential complements to one another, and that whether expressed through the more condensed approach of the Bible, or through the more elaborate approach of the New Thought, the authentic teaching declares not our independence from God, but our independence within God.

Such an investigation naturally focuses in a special way on the teachings of Jesus; for regardless of what our views may be concerning the nature of the authority with which he spoke, we must all acknowledge that a unique significance belongs to those statements which have been passed down to us as the exact words from which the entire New Testament has been developed; and if a unity of understanding in the New Thought movement can be discovered here at the source, we may anticipate finding it in the subsequent developments as well.

The key to the Master's teaching can be found in his conversation with the Woman of Samaria, and it lies within the statement that "the Father" is Spirit—that is, Spirit in the absolute and unqualified sense of the word, as shown in the original Greek, and not "A Spirit" as it appears in the Authorized Version. Then, as the natural counterpart to "the Father," we find another term used: "the Son." The relationship between these two forms the central subject of Jesus' teaching, and therefore, it is extremely important to have some clear understanding of what he meant by these terms if we want to comprehend what it was that he actually taught.

Now if "the Father" represents Spirit, then "the Son" must also represent Spirit, since a son necessarily shares the same nature as his father. However, since "the Father" is Spirit that is Absolute and Universal, it becomes clear that "the Son" cannot be Spirit that is Absolute and Universal, because two Universal Spirits cannot exist simultaneously—if there were two, neither would truly be universal. We can therefore logically conclude that because "the Father" is Universal Spirit, "the Son" is Spirit that is not universal; and the only way to define Spirit that is not universal is as Spirit that has been individualized and made particular. Scripture teaches us that "the Spirit is Life," and using this as our definition of "Spirit," we discover that "the Father" is Absolute, Originating, Undifferentiated Life, while "the Son" is this same Life differentiated into specific forms. Therefore, in the broadest sense of the term, "the Son" represents all of creation, whether visible or invisible, and in this sense it is simply the differentiation of universal Life into countless particular expressions. But if we possess any meaningful understanding of the intelligent and responsive nature of Spirit—if we recognize that because it is Pure Being it must be Infinite Intelligence and Infinite Responsiveness—then we will understand that its manifestation in the particular allows for countless degrees, ranging from simple expression as outward form all the way up to the fullest possible expression of the infinite intelligence and responsiveness that Spirit truly is.

The teachings of Jesus spoke directly to people's hearts and minds, so when he talked about becoming sons of God, he was referring to how Infinite Being expresses itself through human hearts and intellects. This concept can be understood in countless degrees of development. Some people have only the basic potential for this spiritual sonship, which remains completely undeveloped. Others show the early signs of its growth, while still others demonstrate more advanced development, and this progression continues until we can imagine a supreme example where someone achieves the absolutely perfect reflection of the universal. Each of these stages represents a deeper and more complete expression of sonship, with the highest development reaching a level that can only be described as the perfect image of "the Father." This represents the natural outcome of continuous growth from an inner principle of Life that forms the core identity of every individual.

It is therefore a necessary conclusion from Jesus' own explanation of "the Father" as Spirit or Infinite Being that "the Son" represents the Biblical term for the manifestation of Infinite Being within the individual, viewed at that point where the person begins to some degree to recognize their unity with their original source, or at least where they possess the capacity for such recognition, even if the actual awareness has not yet occurred. It is quite striking that, by defining "the Son" based on Jesus' direct statement, we reach precisely the same definition of Spirit as "that power which knows itself." The potential reality of sonship lies in this capacity to recognize one's shared nature with "the Father," for the prodigal son remained a son even before he started to understand his relationship to his "Father" in reality. The emergence of this awareness creates the spiritual "babe," or infant son; and gradually this consciousness develops until he reaches the complete state of spiritual maturity. This recognition by the individual of their own unity with Universal Spirit forms exactly the foundation of the New Thought; and therefore from the beginning both systems emerge from a shared center.

But I believe the aspect of New Thought that presents the biggest obstacle to those who observe the movement from the outside is its assertion that thought-power serves as an active force in everyday life. As simply a collection of theoretical ideas, people might be willing to categorize it alongside the philosophical systems of Kant or Hegel; however, it's the practical component that creates the problem. It's not merely a system of thought founded on the concept of the Unity of Being, but it asserts that this concept should be carried through to its logical conclusions in creating visible and concrete external outcomes through the simple use of thought-power. An absurd assertion, a claim that common sense cannot accept, an invasion of Divine authority, a declaration of unprecedented boldness: so says the casual critic. Yet this assertion is not without precedent, for the same claim was made on the same foundation by the Great Teacher Himself as the natural outcome of "the Son's" understanding of his relationship to "the Father." "Ask what ye will, and it shall be done unto you"; "Whatsoever you shall ask in prayer, believing, you shall receive, and nothing shall be impossible unto you"; "All things are possible to him that believeth." These declarations are completely without any restriction except that created by the seeker's lack of faith in his own ability to influence the Infinite. This is as clear a statement of the power of mental force to create outward and concrete results as any currently made by New Thought, and it's made on exactly the same foundation, specifically, the willingness of "the Father" or Spirit in the Universal to respond to the activity of Spirit in the individual.

In the Bible, this movement of individualized Spirit is called "prayer," and it means the same thing as Thought that's deliberately formed with the purpose of creating this response.

"Prayer is the heart's sincere desire,

"Whether spoken aloud or kept silent,"

and we must not let ourselves be misled by connecting specific forms with specific words, but should follow the wise advice of Oliver Wendell Holmes, and put such words through a process of depolarization, which reveals their true meaning. Whether we call our action "prayer" or "thought-concentration," we mean the same thing; it is the assertion of the person to influence the Infinite through the power of his own mind.

Some might argue that this definition leaves out a crucial aspect of prayer—the question of whether God will actually hear it. However, this is precisely the element that Jesus most strictly removes from his description of this mental process. Prayer, as most people understand it, is highly uncertain. Whether our prayers will be answered depends entirely on another's will, and since we know nothing about how that will operates, popular belief holds that uncertainty is the very heart of prayer. Jesus viewed prayer in completely the opposite way. He tells us to believe that we have already received what we're asking for, and he makes this belief the requirement for actually receiving it. In other words, he makes the key component of this mental action complete certainty about the corresponding response from the Infinite, which is exactly the same condition that New Thought establishes for the effective use of Thought-power.

It might be argued, however, that if people possess this unlimited ability to direct their thoughts toward achieving whatever they want, they can use this power for harmful purposes just as easily as for beneficial ones. But Jesus fully understood this possibility and performed the only destructive miracle attributed to him specifically to highlight this danger. The explanation provided by the Gospel writers for the destruction of the fig tree is clearly insufficient, since we certainly cannot imagine Jesus being so unreasonable as to curse a tree for not producing fruit when it was out of season. However, the account itself reveals a very different intention. Jesus responded to his disciples' amazed questions by telling them that they had the power not only to do what had been done to the fig tree, but to create effects on a much larger scale; and he ended the conversation by establishing the requirement of deep, forgiving examination of the heart as an essential prerequisite to prayer. Why was this teaching so specifically emphasized in this particular context? Clearly because the demonstration he had just provided of the power of directed thought in the hands of trained individuals revealed that this ability can be used for destruction as well as for benefit, and that, consequently, a thorough examination of the heart to eliminate any hidden resentment became an essential prerequisite for its safe application; otherwise there was risk of harmful thought-forces being unleashed to harm others. The miracle of the fig tree served as a practical lesson to demonstrate the need for careful management of that unlimited power which Jesus assured his disciples existed as completely in them as it did in himself. I do not attempt to explore this topic in detail here, but enough has, I believe, been demonstrated to persuade us that Jesus made precisely the same assertion about the power of Thought as that made by the New Thought movement today. It is a significant claim, and it is, therefore, reassuring to find such an authority supporting the same statement.

The fundamental principle that New Thought advocates use to support this claim is the identity of Spirit in the individual with spirit in the universal, and we will discover that this also forms the foundation of Jesus' teaching on this subject. He states that "the Son can do nothing of himself, but what he seeth the Father do these things doeth the Son in like manner." It should now be clear enough that "the Son" is a general term, not limited to one specific person, but applicable to everyone; and this statement explains how "the Son" works in relationship to "the Father." The key point this sentence emphasizes is that what the Son does corresponds to what he sees the Father doing. His actions match his perception. When his perception expands, his actions expand accordingly. However, we are all familiar enough with this principle in other areas. What sets apart an Edison or a Marconi from an apprentice who only knows how to install an electric bell by following basic instructions? It is their ability to see the universal principles of electricity and apply them to specific situations. The great painter is someone who sees the universal principles of form and color where a lesser artist sees only a specific combination; and the same applies to the great surgeon, the great chemist, the great lawyer—in every field it is the power of insight that distinguishes the great person from the ordinary one; it is the ability to make broad generalizations and perceive far-reaching laws that elevates the exceptional mind above the common level. Greater achievement always comes from deeper understanding of the abstract principles from which any art or science originates; and this same law applied to the universal principles of Life is the law by which "the Son's" work is proportioned to his understanding of "the Father's" methods. Therefore the source of "the Son's" power lies in contemplating "the Father," which means the effort to understand the true nature of Being, whether in abstract form or in its general patterns of manifestation. This is Bacon's principle, "Work as God works"; and similarly the New Thought consists above all else in understanding the laws of Being.

The outcome of this perception is that "the Son" performs the same actions as "the Father" "in the same way." The Son's work involves applying universal principles to particular situations. These principles stay unchanged and always operate in the same manner, and "the Son's" role is to identify the specific area where these principles will work in relation to the particular object he is focusing on; therefore, regarding that object, the action of "the Son" also becomes the action of "the Father."

Once again, "the Father" keeps nothing hidden. He holds no secrets, because "the Father loveth the Son, and showeth him all things that himself doeth." There exists perfect mutual exchange between Spirit in its Universal form and in its Individual expression, stemming from their identical essence. When "the Son" recognizes Love as the driving force behind this Unity, he gains an instinctive understanding of all the hidden mechanisms of Universal Life that we refer to as Nature's mysteries. Love possesses a divine capacity for insight that intellect by itself cannot achieve, and the ancient saying, "Love will find out the way," contains far deeper meaning than what appears on its surface. Therefore, there is not merely a seeing, but also a revealing. The three elements—"looking, seeing, showing"—unite to create a power of "working" that has no boundaries we can define.

Here, once again, the teaching of Jesus aligns perfectly with that of the New Thought, which tells us that limitations exist only where we place them ourselves, and that viewing ourselves as beings of unlimited knowledge, power, and love means becoming exactly that in the outward expression of visible reality. Any criticism, therefore, of the New Thought teaching about the possibilities hidden within humanity applies with equal strength to the teachings of Jesus. His teaching clearly stated that the perfect individuality of humanity is a Dual-Unity, the polarization of the Infinite in the Manifest; and it requires only the recognition of this truth for the manifested element in this dual system to demonstrate its identity with the corresponding element that remains externally invisible. He said that He and his Father were One, that those who had seen him had seen the Father, that the words he spoke were the Father's, and that it was the Father who performed the works. Nothing could be more clear. Complete unity of the manifested individuality with the Originating Infinite Spirit is declared or suggested in every statement attributed to Jesus, whether spoken about himself or about others. He recognizes only one fundamental difference, the difference between those who understand this truth and those who do not understand it. The distinction between the disciple and the master is one only of degree, which will be erased by the expansive power of growth; "the disciple, when he is perfected, shall be as his Master."

The only thing that prevents a person from using the complete power of the Infinite for any purpose is their lack of faith—their failure to fully understand the incredible truth that they themselves are the very power they're looking for. This was Jesus's teaching, just as it is the teaching of the New Thought; and once this truth of humanity's Divine Sonship is accepted as the fundamental foundation, a magnificent structure of possibilities that "eye hath not seen, nor ear heard, neither hath entered into the heart of man to conceive," develops logically from it—a glorious inheritance that everyone can rightfully claim simply by virtue of being human.

Intelligence and Responsiveness represent the fundamental nature of Spirit in every form, and when this essence concentrates into centers of consciousness, it creates personality—that is, self-aware individuality. This quality varies tremendously in intensity, ranging from its earliest hints in animals to its profound development in the Great Masters of Spiritual Science. For this reason, it's known as "The Power that Knows Itself"—it's the ability of Self-recognition that forms personality, and as we come to understand that our personality isn't entirely contained between our hat and our boots, as Walt Whitman puts it, but extends outward into the Infinite, which we then discover to be the Infinite within ourselves, the same I AM that I am, our personality expands and we become aware of ever-greater levels of Life within ourselves.

Everything depends on this principle of Reciprocity. Through contemplation we come to understand the true nature of "Spirit" or "the father." We learn to separate the changing factors of specific Modes from the unchanging factors which are the essential qualities of Spirit that underlie all Modes. When we recognize these essential qualities we see that we can apply them under any mode that we choose: in other words we provide the variable factor of the combination through the action of our Thought, as Desire or Will, and thus combine it with the unchanging factor or "constant" of the essential law of spirit, thereby producing whatever result we desire. This is exactly what we do in relation to physical nature—for example, the electrician provides the variable factor of the particular Mode of application, and the constant laws of Electricity respond to the nature of the invitation given to them. This Responsiveness is inherent in Spirit; otherwise Spirit would have no means of expansion into manifestation. Responsiveness is the principle of Spirit's Self-expression. We do not have to create responsive action on the part of electricity. We can safely take this Responsiveness for granted as pure natural law. Our desire first works on the Arupa level and then concentrates itself through the various Rupa levels until it reaches complete external manifestation.

Chapter 2: The Great Affirmation

I assume that my readers are already familiar with the role that the principle of Affirmation plays in the New Thought system. This concept often creates difficulties for newcomers, and I'm confident that even experienced practitioners will appreciate any help in gaining a deeper understanding of this fundamental truth. Therefore, I intend to explore what the Bible teaches about this significant topic.

The stated purpose of the Bible is to establish and spread "the Kingdom of God" across the entire world, and this can only be accomplished by repeating the same process from one person to another, until the entire population is transformed. This is therefore an individual process; and, as we discovered in the previous chapter, God is Spirit and Spirit is Life, and consequently, the growth of "the Kingdom of God" means the growth of the principle of Life within each person. Now Life, to truly be life, must be Affirmative. It is Life because of what it is, and not because of what it is not. The amount of life in any specific instance may be quite small; but, no matter how small the quantity, the quality remains always the same: it is the quality of Being, the quality of Livingness, and not its absence, that makes it what it is. The distinguishing characteristic of Life, therefore, is that it is Positive and not Negative; and every degree of negativeness, that is, every limitation, can ultimately be traced back to a deficiency of Life-power.

Limitations surround us because we believe we're unable to do what we want. Every time we say "I cannot," we hit a wall of limitation and stop using our mental power in that direction because we think we're blocked by an impossible barrier. When this happens, we become trapped. The ideal of perfect freedom is the opposite of all this and follows a different path that doesn't lead us into a dead end. This path consists of three statements: I am—therefore I can—therefore I will. This final statement results in directing our abilities, whether inner or outer, toward achieving what we desire. But this last statement has its foundation in the first one. It's because we recognize the positive nature of the life that exists within us, or rather the life that we are, that the power to will or act positively exists at all. Therefore, the extent of our power to will and act positively and effectively is exactly measured by how deeply we understand the depth and vitality of our own existence. The more completely we learn to affirm this truth, the greater power we can exercise.

Now the ideal of perfect Liberty is the complete absence of all limitation, and to have no limitation in Being is to be co-extensive with All-Being. We are all grammarians enough to know that the use of a predicate is to lead the mind to contemplate the subject as represented by that predicate; in other words, it limits our conception for the time being to that particular aspect of the subject. Hence every predicate, however extensive, implies some limitation of the subject. But the ideal subject, the absolutely free self, is, by the very hypothesis, without limitation; and, therefore, no predicate can be attached to it. It stands as a declaration of its own Being without any statement of what that Being consists in, and therefore it says of itself, not "I am this or that," but simply I am. No predicate can be added, because the only commensurate predicate would be the enumeration of Infinity. Therefore, both logically and grammatically, the only possible statement of a fully liberated being is made in the words I am.

I hardly need to remind my readers how often Jesus used these powerful words. In many instances, translators have added the word "He," but they have been careful to put it in italics to show that it doesn't appear in the original text. As scholars of grammar and theology, they felt something more was needed to complete the meaning, and they added it accordingly. However, if we want to understand the exact words as the Master himself spoke them, we must remove this addition. Once we do this, the connection between his statement and the one made to Moses at the burning bush immediately becomes clear, where the full meaning of the words is so evident that the translators were forced to leave the predicate's position in that apparent emptiness which comes from filling all things.

Viewed in this way, a wonderful light emerges from the teachings of the Great Teacher: regardless of how we might consider him as a Great Exception to the weak and limited nature of humanity that we know all too well, we must all acknowledge that his purpose was not to make mankind lose hope by declaring that the path of progress was blocked to them, but "to give light to them that sit in darkness," and freedom to those who are enslaved, by announcing the boundless possibilities that exist within man, waiting only to be awakened through knowledge of the Truth. And if we assume any personal meaning in his words, it can therefore only be as the Great Example of what man has the potential to become, and not as the example of something which man can never aspire to be; an Exception, indeed, to humanity as we observe them today, but the Exception that proves the rule, and establishes the standard of what each person may become as he reaches the measure of the stature of the fullness of Christ.

Let us, therefore, remove this added text and restore the Master's words as they appear in the original: "Unless you believe that I am, you will die in your sins." This summarizes his entire teaching.

"The last enemy that shall be overcome is death," and the "sting," or deadly power, of death is "sin." Take that away, and death no longer has any control over us; its power comes to an end. And "the strength of sin is the Law": sin represents every violation of the law of Being; and the law of Being is infinitude; for Being is Life, and Life in its deepest essence is the unlimited I am. Dying in our sins is therefore not a punishment for questioning a specific theological doctrine, but it is the inevitable natural result of not understanding, not believing in, the I am. As long as we fail to recognize its complete infinitude within ourselves, we separate ourselves from our conscious unity with the Infinite Life-Spirit that flows through all things. Without this principle we have no choice but to die—and this happens because of our sin, that is, because of our failure to align with the true Law of our Being, which is Life, and not Death. We declare Death and Negation about ourselves, and therefore Death and Negation are made manifest, and thus we pay the price of not believing in the fundamental Law of our own Life, which is the Law of all Life. The Bible is the Book of Principles, and therefore by "dying" is meant the acceptance of the principle of the Negative which reaches its peak in Death as the complete sum of all limitations, and which brings at every step those restrictions which are of the nature of Death, because their tendency is to limit the outpouring abundance of Life.

This, then, represents the core essence of Jesus's teaching: that our lack of faith in the unlimited power of Life within ourselves— within each one of us—stands as the single cause of Death and all those harmful forces that, to varying degrees, mirror the limiting influences that rob Life of its completeness and happiness. To escape Death and step into Life, each of us must believe in the I am within ourselves. What foundation supports this belief? Simply that no other possibility makes sense. If our life doesn't represent a part of Universal Spirit's life, where else could it come from? We exist because that exists. No other explanation works. The complete affirmation of our own aliveness isn't bold self-promotion: it's the only reasonable conclusion we can draw from the fact that life exists anywhere at all, and that we're here to contemplate it. In terms of Universal Being, only One I am can exist, and when individuals understand and use these words properly, they're declaring this truth. The forms through which this manifests are endless, but the Life being manifested remains One, so every person who recognizes this truth about themselves discovers in the I am both their individual self and the wholeness of everything that exists; this leads them to understand that when they tap into the inner nature of the things and people around them, they're actually using the powers of their own life.

Sometimes the veil that Jesus placed over this profound truth was quite transparent. To the Samaritan woman, he described it as a spring of Life continuously flowing up from the deepest parts of human existence; and later, to the crowd gathered at the Temple, he portrayed it as a river of Life constantly streaming from the hidden sources of the spirit within us. For Life to truly belong to us, it must be who we are. An energy that merely flowed through us without becoming part of us might create some kind of mechanical activity, but it wouldn't be genuine Life. Life can never exist as something separate from the individual who expresses it; therefore, even if we imagine the life-principle in a person becoming so powerful that it throbs with what might appear to us as completely divine energy, it would still be nothing other than that person themselves. In this way, Jesus points us toward no outside source of life, but consistently teaches that the Kingdom of Heaven exists within, and that what we need is to tear down those walls of ignorance and hostility that stop us from understanding that the great I am, which is the deepest Spirit of Life throughout the universe, is the same I am that I am, regardless of who I might be.

On another memorable occasion Jesus declared again that the I am is the enduring principle of Life. It is this that is the Resurrection and the Life; not, as Martha supposed, a new principle to be infused from without at some future time, but an inherent core of vitality awaiting only its own recognition of itself to triumph over death and the grave. And yet, again hear the Master's answer to the inquiring Thomas. How many of us, like him, desire to know the way! To hear of wonderful powers latent in man and requiring only development is beautiful and hopeful, if we could only find out the way to develop them; but who will show us the way? The answer comes with no uncertain note. The I am includes everything. It is at once "the Way, the Truth, and the Life": not the Life only, or the Truth only, but also the Way by which to reach them. Can words be plainer? It is by continually affirming and relying on the I am in ourselves as identical with the I am that is the One and Only Life, whether manifested or unmanifested, in all places of the universe, that we shall find the way to the attainment of all Truth and of all Life. Here we have the predicate which we are seeking to complete our affirmation regarding ourselves. I am—what? the Three things which include all things: Truth, which is all Knowledge and Wisdom; Life, which is all Power and Love; and the unfailing Way which will lead us step by step, if we follow it, to heights too sublime and environment too wide for our present juvenile imaginings to picture.

As the New Testament centers around Jesus, the Old Testament centers around Moses, and he also declares the Great Affirmation to be the same. For him God has no name, but represents that intensely living universal Life which encompasses everything, and no name could adequately capture its essence. The emphatic words "I am" are the only possible statement of the One-Power that manifests itself as all worlds and all living beings. It is the Great "I am" that forever unfolds itself in all the infinite evolutionary forces of the cosmic design, and which, in its marvelous forward progression, develops itself into higher and higher conscious intelligence in the successive races of humanity, revealing the scroll of history as it advances from age to age, working out with perfect precision the steady forward movement of everything toward that ultimate perfection in which God's work will be completed. But magnificent as is the scale on which this Providential Power reveals itself to Moses and the Prophets, it remains nothing other than the very same Power that Jesus encourages us to realize within ourselves.

The scope of its work can be expanded to the grand scale of world history, or narrowed down to focus on a single person: the difference is simply a matter of size; but the Life-principle remains constant. It is always the principle of confident Affirmation based on the peaceful understanding that all things are simply expressions of itself, and that, as a result, everything must move together in one powerful unity that allows no conflicting elements. Once this "unity of the spirit" is clearly understood, to say I am is to send the vibrations of our thought-currents throughout the universe to carry out our commands when and where we choose; and, in the same way, it is to draw in the life-giving influences of Infinite Spirit as if from an endless ocean of Life, which can never be depleted and from which no force can prevent us. And all of this is true because it is the highest law of Nature. It is not the introduction of a new system, but simply the allowing of the original and only possible system to continue on to its rightful completion. A Divine Order, indeed, but we will find nothing anywhere that is not Divine; and it is to the understanding of this Divine and Living Order that the Bible aims to guide us. But we will never experience it around us until we first experience it within us. We can see God outside only through the light of God inside; and this light grows stronger as we become aware of the Divine nature of the innermost I am which is the center of our own individuality.

Therefore, Jesus tells us that the "I am" is "the door." It represents the central point of our individual existence that opens into the unlimited Life of the Infinite. If we want to understand the ancient teaching "know thyself," we must focus our thoughts more and more deeply on our own inner Life until we reach its central radiating point. There we will discover that the door into the Infinite has truly opened to us, and we can move from the deepest part of our own Being into the deepest part of All-Being. This is why Jesus spoke of "the door" as something we should pass through, going in and out to find pasture. Pasture—the nourishment of every ability with its proper sustenance—can be found both within and without. The vitality of Life consists of both concentration and expression: it is not the lifeless balance of inactivity, but the living balance of a vital and rhythmic pulse. Involution and evolution must always alternate, and the door of communication between them is the "I am," which is the living power in both. This is why the Great Affirmation is the Secret of Life, and why saying "I am" with a true understanding of everything it means places us in contact with all the powers of the Infinite.

This is the Universal and Eternal Affirmation that stands without any conditions attached to it; and all specific affirmations can be understood as particular expressions of this all-encompassing truth. I desire this or that specific thing because I understand that I can manifest it in the physical world, and I understand that I can because I know that I exist, and so we continually return to the fundamental central Affirmation of All-Being. Study the Scriptures and you will discover that from beginning to end they teach only this: that every human soul represents an individual expression of that Universal Being, or All-Spirit, which we call God, and that Spirit can never be stripped of its abilities, but like Fire, which serves as its symbol, must always remain completely and perfectly itself, which is Life in all its boundless fullness.

In giving Affirmation the significance it does, the New Thought movement aligns with the teachings of Jesus and Moses and the entire Bible. The reason for this is straightforward. There exists only one Truth, so sincere searching can only lead people to this same Truth, whether they are biblical writers or anyone else. The Bible gets its authority from the inherent truth of what it describes, not the other way around; if these things are true at all, they would remain equally true even if no Bible had ever been written. However, using the Great Affirmation as our foundation, we will discover that the system the Bible teaches is scientific and logical in every aspect, so any other system that is scientifically accurate will match it in essence, regardless of how different it might appear in presentation; therefore, when New Thought advocates discuss the power of Affirmation, they are not promoting some modern nonsense, but simply restating a profound truth that has existed in the world, though very poorly understood, for thousands of years.

The Old Testament and the New Testament approach the I AM from completely different perspectives. The Old Testament examines it through the relationship of the Whole to the Part, while the New Testament examines it through the relationship of the Part to the Whole. This distinction is crucial for understanding how the Old and New Testaments relate to each other.

"My Word shall not return unto me void but shall accomplish that whereunto I send it."

The principle described here involves the alternation and balance between absorption and radiation—taking something in first, then giving it out.

"Order"—Anything that undermines this is "Disorder."

"Conscious"—The level of awareness we possess always signals our movement from a lower to a higher Power of Life. The

Life of All Seven Principles must constantly exist within us, or we would cease to exist entirely; therefore, it is the extent to which we learn to consciously operate within each of these principles that indicates our progression into higher realms within ourselves, and often beyond ourselves as well.

The Central Radiating Point of our Individuality is One with All-Being.

(f) Equilibrium—Notice the distinction between the Living Equilibrium of Alternating Rhythmic Pulsation (the complete Pulsation Doctrine) and the lifeless equilibrium of simply declining to a static state. The first concept involves the Doctrine of the Return, where the Upward Arc balances the Downward Arc—The lifelessness of the second results from the lack of any such balancing force. The Upward Arc emerges from contemplating the Highest Ideal.

Spirit cannot abandon any aspect of its essential nature. It must always contain all the qualities of Spirit within itself, even when the lower aspects of individual consciousness have not yet become aware of this truth.

The Great Affirmation serves as the guide to the entire subject.

Chapter 3: The Father

If, as we have seen, "the Son" represents the principle of Spirit that creates differences, giving birth to countless individual beings, "the Father" represents the unifying principle that binds these countless individuals together into one shared life. The need to recognize this great foundation of universal harmony forms the basis of Jesus' teaching about worship. "Woman, believe me, the hour is coming when you will worship the Father neither on this mountain nor in Jerusalem. You worship what you do not know; we worship what we know, for salvation comes from the Jews. But the hour is coming, and is now here, when the true worshipers will worship the Father in spirit and truth" (Revised Version). In these few words, the Great Teacher summarizes the entire subject. He places particular emphasis on the type of worship he means. Above all else, it is based on knowledge.

"We worship that which we know," and it is this knowledge that gives our worship a healthy and life-giving quality. This isn't the ignorant worship born of wonder and fear—a simple humbling of ourselves before some enormous, unclear, unknown force that might harm us if we don't figure out how to appease it. Instead, it's a specific action carried out with a clear purpose, meaning it's the use of one of our natural abilities directed toward its proper target in an intelligent way. The ignorant Samaritan worship is still better than no worship at all, because at least it recognizes that some center should exist around which a person's life ought to revolve—something to prevent the purposeless scattering of their powers due to the lack of a unifying force to hold them together. Even the most basic understanding of prayer, as simply trying to convince God to change his mind, is at least a first step toward the truth that complete provision for all our needs can be drawn from the Infinite. Nevertheless, worship like this is burdened with confusion and can only provide a weak response to the atheistic mockery that asks, "What is man, that God should be mindful of him, a fleeting speck among countless worlds?"

Now Jesus's teaching sweeps away all these confusions with a single word: "knowledge." There's only one correct way to accomplish anything, and that means knowing precisely what we want to achieve and understanding exactly why we want to achieve it. Every other approach is simply stumbling around in the dark. We might accidentally stumble upon the right answer sometimes, but we can't build our entire life around this hit-or-miss approach for all eternity. If we'll eventually have to abandon this fumbling method anyway, why not abandon it right now and immediately start benefiting from acting according to clear, understandable principles? Understanding that "the Son," as individualized Spirit, has his corresponding counterpart in "the Father," as Universal Spirit, provides us with the key we need.

In whatever way we might try to explain it, the fact remains that will is the fundamental characteristic of Spirit. We can speak of conscious, subconscious, or superconscious action; but however we might picture the condition of the agent contemplating their own action, a general purposeful life-affirming tendency becomes abundantly clear when we take any broad view of Nature, whether observed from the outside or from within, and we can call this by the general name of will. But the mistake we must avoid is assuming that will takes the same form in Universal Spirit as it does in individualized Spirit. The very terms "universal" and "individual" prevent this. For the universal, as such, to exercise specific will, focusing itself on the details of a particular case, would mean it passes into individualization and ceases to be the Absolute and Infinite; it would no longer be "the Father," but "the Son." It is therefore precisely by not exercising specific will that "the Father" remains "the Father," or the Great Unifying Principle. But the volitional quality is not absent from Spirit in the Universal for this reason; otherwise, where would that quality appear in ourselves? It is present; but according to the nature of the plane on which it operates. The Universal is not the Specific, and everything on the plane of the Universal must share in the nature of that plane. Therefore, will in "the Father" is not specific; and that which is not specific and individual must be generic. Generic will, then, is that mode of will which belongs to the Universal, and generic will is tendency. This is the solution to the puzzle, and this solution is given, not obscurely, in Jesus' statement that "the Father" seeks those true worshippers who worship Him in spirit and in truth.

What exactly do we mean when we talk about tendency? The word comes from the Latin root "tendere," which means to stretch.

It describes a force pushing outward in a specific direction—the tension created when some power tries to expand itself. But what kind of force are we talking about? It's the Universal Life-Principle, because "the Spirit is Life." Using the language of modern science, this "seeking" behavior from "the Father" represents the expansive pressure of the Universal Life-Principle as it looks for the path of least resistance. This is the route through which it can flow into the fullest expression of individualized Life. This tendency will manifest in physical form based on how much reception it encounters.

St. John says, "This is the boldness that we have towards him, that if we ask anything according to His will, He heareth us; and if we know that He heareth us whatsoever we ask, we know that we have the petitions that we have asked of Him" (1 John v. 14). However, when we follow the common understanding of "the will of God," this passage completely loses its meaning, because it makes everything dependent on our asking "according to His will," and if we begin with the concept of an individual act of Divine choice in each separate situation, nothing less than a special revelation constantly repeated could tell us what the Divine will was in each specific case. When seen from this perspective, this passage becomes nothing more than a mockery of our limitations. But once we understand that "the will of God" is an unchanging law of tendency, we have a clear standard by which to determine whether we can rightfully expect to receive what we want. We can examine this law of tendency just as we would study any other law, and it is this examination that forms the heart of genuine worship.

The word "worship" means to consider something worthy; to consider it worthy, that is, of careful attention. The saying goes that "imitation is the sincerest form of flattery," but more accurately we could say that it represents the most genuine form of worship. Therefore, true worship involves studying the Universal Life-Principle "the Father," examining both its essential nature and how it operates; and once we have come to understand "the Law of God," the law that exists within the very nature of Infinite Being, we will discover that by aligning our own individual actions with this universal law, we will find that this law will consistently produce the outcomes we seek. This process is no more or less miraculous than what happens in any application of scientific principles. Only the true chemist or engineer who first masters how to work with the fundamental tendencies of natural laws can then direct them toward achieving his personal objectives; no other approach will work. The same principle applies to the student of life's divine mystery. He must first understand the great laws governing its fundamental tendencies, and then he will be equipped to apply that tendency toward creating any specific result he desires.

Common sense shows us what the law of this tendency must be. The Master taught that a house divided against itself cannot stand; and for the Life-Principle to do anything that restricts the fullest expansion of life would be for it to act toward its own destruction. The test, therefore, in every case, whether our intention falls within the scope of the great law, is this: Does it operate for the expansion or for the restriction of life? According to the answer, we can say positively whether or not our purpose aligns with "the will of God." Therefore, as long as we work within the scope of this universal "will of the Father," we need have no fear of the Divine Providence, as an agency, acting against us. We may dismiss this fear, for we ourselves are manifestations of the very power which we call "the Father." The I am is one; and as long as we preserve this unity by conforming to the universal nature of the I am, it will certainly never destroy the unity by entering upon a specific course of action on its own account.

Here, then, we discover the secret of power. It lies in the genuine worship of "the Father," which means constantly recognizing that Originating Spirit gives life, and understanding that we, as individuals, remain parts of that Spirit. Therefore, the law of our nature is to continuously draw life from the endless reserves of the Infinite—not bottles of life-giving water mixed with other substances and labeled for specific purposes, but the complete flow of the pure stream itself, which we are free to use for any purpose we choose. "Whoever desires it, let him take the water of life freely." This is how the worship of "the Father" becomes the central principle of individual life, not by limiting our freedom, but by providing the only possible foundation for it. Just as a planetary system would be impossible without a central controlling sun, harmonious life is impossible without recognizing Infinite Spirit as that Power whose natural tendency guides each individual being into its proper orbit. This is what the Bible teaches, and it is also what the New Thought teaches, which states that life with all its unlimited possibilities is a continuous outflow from the Infinite that we may direct in any way we choose.

But you might wonder, what happens if we go against this fundamental law of Spirit? This is an important question, and I must leave the answer for further consideration.

Chapter 4: Conclusion

I ended my last chapter with the crucial question: What happens when we go against the fundamental law of Spirit? What occurs when we oppose any natural law? Clearly, the law works against us. We can utilize Nature's laws, but we cannot change them. When we resist any natural law, we put ourselves in an upside-down relationship with it, and consequently, from this mistaken perspective, it seems as if the law itself were deliberately working against us. However, this reversal comes entirely from us, not from any modification in how the law operates. The law of Spirit, like all other natural laws, is inherently impersonal; but we project into it, in a sense, the mirror image of our own personality, though we cannot change its fundamental nature; and therefore, if we resist its basic tendency toward universal good, we will discover in it the reflection of our own resistance and stubbornness.

The law of Spirit moves forward unchangeably on its path, and what people commonly refer to as Divine wrath is simply the natural reaction that occurs when we place ourselves in conflict with this law. The harm that follows is not a personal intervention by the Universal Spirit, which would mean it was taking specific form, but rather the natural result of the causes we have set in motion ourselves. However, the impact on us will be exactly the same as if these effects were caused by the deliberate action of a hostile personality, even though we may not recognize that the personal element is actually our own. And if we have any understanding of the remarkably complex nature of humanity, and the various interconnected principles that connect the physical body at one end of the spectrum to the purely spiritual Self at the other, we will have some small sense of the enormous scope on which these negative influences can work, not being limited to the level of external manifestation, but operating equally on those inner levels that give birth to the outer world and are of a more lasting character.

Therefore, the philosophical study of Spirit, rather than providing any justification for loose behavior, gives strong emphasis to the biblical command to escape from God's anger. However, it also frees us from unfounded fears—the worry that our repentance might not be accepted, the concern that we might be turned away because we cannot agree with some traditional religious doctrine, the anxiety of complete uncertainty about what lies ahead. These fears make life miserable and the thought of death terrifying for those who are enslaved by them. Understanding that we are working with a force that treats everyone equally, one that never changes and is actually an unchangeable Law, immediately sets us free from all these fears.

The unchanging nature of Law guarantees that no amount of previous resistance to it, whether stemming from ignorance or stubbornness, will stop it from operating according to its own beneficial and life-giving nature once we abandon our backward position and establish ourselves in proper relationship with it. Natural laws don't hold grudges; once we align our approaches with their character, they will work in our favor without looking back at our past mistakes. The law of Spirit might be more intricate than the law of electricity, since it expresses itself through us as the law of conscious individuality; however, it remains a completely natural law that follows the universal principle, and therefore we can dismiss from our thoughts, as a groundless fantasy, any fear of Divine power storing up wrath against us because of past events, provided we are genuinely trying to do what is right in the present moment. The new causes we set in motion today will generate their appropriate results just as certainly as the old causes did; by starting a new chain of good actions, we will break the old chain of harmful ones. However, we obviously cannot expect to create this new sequence while we continue repeating the old causes, since the outcome must inevitably reflect the nature of what we plant. Therefore, we control our circumstances, and whether in this life or the next, it is up to us to either continue the harm or eliminate it and replace it with good. It's worth noting in passing that the central Christian doctrine rests on the most complete understanding of this law and represents the practical application of the deepest psychological science to a profound problem. But this is an extensive topic that cannot be properly addressed here.

Much has been written and said about where evil comes from, and an entire book could be filled with a detailed examination of this topic; but for all practical purposes, it can be summarized in one word: limitation. What is the root cause of all conflict, whether public or private, other than the belief that the supply of good things is limited? For most people, this is a deeply held belief, and they therefore reason that because there is only a certain limited amount of good available, their share can only be increased by reducing someone else's portion accordingly. Anyone who holds this same belief naturally resents any attempt to take away part of this limited supply; and this gives rise to the entire range of envy, hatred, fraud, and violence, whether between individuals, social classes, or nations. If people could only understand the truth that "good" is not some fixed, limited quantity, but rather a stream that flows continuously from the inexhaustible Infinite, ready to move in whatever direction we choose to guide it, and that each person can draw from it endlessly through the power of their own thoughts, replacing this old and false idea of limitation with this new and true understanding would instantly eliminate all conflict and struggle from the world; every person would discover an ally rather than a rival in every other person, and the very laws of Nature, which now so often appear to work against us, would prove to be an endless source of benefit and joy.

"They could not enter into rest because of unbelief," "they limited the Holy One of Israel": in these words the Bible, like New Thought, traces all the world's sorrow—that terrible sense of world-weariness which expresses itself with such devastating influence through today's pessimistic literature—to the single root of a false belief, the belief in humanity's limitations. Simply replace it with the true belief, and the evil would come to an end. Now the foundation of this true belief is that clear understanding of "the Father" which, as I have demonstrated, forms the basis of Jesus' teaching. If, from one perspective, the Intelligent Universal Life-Principle is a Power to be obeyed, in the same way that we must obey all the laws of Nature, from the opposite perspective, it is a power to be utilized. We must never lose sight of the fact that obedience to any natural law in its general tendency necessarily brings with it a corresponding power of using that law in specific application. This is the old saying that knowledge is power. It is the old paradox with which Jesus challenged the ignorant scribes about how David's Lord could also be his Son. The word "David" means "Beloved" and to be beloved implies that mutual sympathy which is intuitive knowledge. Therefore David, the Beloved, is the person who has realized his true relationship as a Son to his Father and who is "in tune with the Infinite." On one hand, this "Infinite" is his "Lord" because it is the combination of all those unchangeable Laws from which it is impossible to deviate without suffering consequent loss of power; and on the other hand, this knowledge of the innermost principles of All-Being puts him in possession of unlimited powers which he can apply to any specific purpose that he chooses; and thus he stands towards them in the position of a father who has authority to command the services of his son. Thus David's "Lord," becomes by a natural transition his "Son."

The principle of "Sonship" lies precisely in this concept. It involves elevating humanity from a state of servitude caused by limitations to the position of a child through the complete elimination of all restrictions. To embrace and live by this principle means to "believe on the Son of God," and a genuine belief in our own sonship liberates us from all harm and from any fear of harm—it transports us from the realm of death into the realm of Life. Like all things, this must develop gradually, but once the beneficial seed of liberating Truth is planted in the heart, it will certainly sprout, and the more we strive to nurture its development by attempting to understand with our minds the reasoning behind these matters and to put our knowledge into practice, the more quickly we will discover our lives growing in vitality—bringing joy to ourselves, light to our households, and blessings that extend to everyone around us in ever-expanding circles.

We've now covered enough ground to demonstrate that the Bible's teachings and New Thought principles are fundamentally the same. If we examined this topic thoroughly, it would require many volumes to explain both the Old and New Testaments in detail, and if such an extensive work were ever undertaken, I'm confident the similarities would be evident down to the smallest details. However, I hope the insights shared in these preceding discussions will be sufficient to demonstrate that these two systems don't conflict with each other—or more accurately, to show that they are actually one unified approach, representing the One Truth that has always existed and always will exist. If what I've attempted to present to my readers inspires any of them to explore this subject more deeply on their own, I can assure them of an endless source of amazement, joy, and empowerment in studying the Old Book through the lens of New Thought.

XX: Jachin and Boaz

"And he erected the pillars in front of the temple, one on the right side, and the other on the left; and he named the one on the right Jachin, and the one on the left Boaz." (II Chronicles 3:17)

Very likely some of us have wondered about the meaning of these two mysterious pillars that Solomon erected in front of his temple, and why they received these strange names; then we've dismissed the topic as one of those unexplainable things passed down in the Bible from ancient times which, we assume, can have no practical relevance for us today. However, these strange names are not without purpose. They hold the key to the entire Bible and to the whole natural order, and as symbols of the two great principles that serve as the pillars of the universe, they appropriately stood at the entrance of that temple which was intended to represent all the mysteries of existence.

In all Semitic languages, the letters J and Y can be used interchangeably, as we observe in modern Arabic where "Yakub" stands for "Jacob" and in ancient Hebrew where "Yaveh" represents "Jehovah." This interchange provides us with the form "Yachin," which immediately solves the mystery. The word Yak means "one," while the ending "hi" or "him" serves as an intensifier that can be translated into English as "only." Therefore, the word "Jachin" breaks down into the words "one only," representing the all-encompassing Unity.

The meaning of Boaz becomes clear when we look at the book of Ruth. In that story, Boaz appears as the relative who exercises the right of pre-emption, a concept well-known to those familiar with Oriental law—a right designed to preserve the Family as the basic social unit. Under this widespread custom, when someone outside the family purchases property, they buy it with the understanding that family members within certain degrees of relationship have the right to buy it back, thereby returning it to the family that originally owned it. Regardless of what our individual views might be concerning the complex questions of doctrinal theology, we can all find common ground regarding the general principle demonstrated in Boaz's actions. He restores the lost estate to the family—in other words, he "redeems" it in the legal meaning of that term. From a legal standpoint, his authority to do this comes from his family membership; however, his motivation for taking this action is love, specifically his affection for Ruth. Without extending the comparison too far, we can say that Boaz represents the principle of redemption in its broadest sense of reclaiming property through family connection, while the deepest driving force behind its recovery is Love.

This is what Boaz represents in the beautiful story of Ruth, and there's no reason we shouldn't allow the same name to represent the same thing when we search for the meaning of the mysterious pillar. Therefore, the two pillars symbolize Unity and the redeeming power of Love, with the meaningful implication that redemption comes from Unity. They align with the two "bonds," or unifying principles that St. Paul spoke about: "the Unity of the Spirit which is the Bond of Peace," and "Love, which is the Bond of Perfectness."

The first represents Unity of Being, while the second represents Unity of Intention. The principle behind this Dual-Unity is perfectly demonstrated through the story of Boaz. The entire narrative is built upon the concept of the Family as the fundamental social unit, which forms the foundational idea of all Oriental law. When we examine the Family from this perspective, we can see how precisely it embodies the dual concept of Jachin and Boaz—unity of Being and unity of Thought. The Family creates a unified whole because all its members descend from a shared ancestor, making them all of the same bloodline. However, while this natural unity of Being cannot be stripped away from them, it alone is insufficient to create a truly united family, as experience sadly demonstrates all too frequently. Something additional is required, and that element is Love. There must be a personal bond created through sympathetic Thought to complete the natural connection that results from birth. The inherent unity must be expressed through the individual choice of each family member, and in this way the Family becomes the ideally perfect social unit. This truth is referenced by St. Paul when he describes God as the Father from Whom every family in heaven and on earth receives its name. Therefore, Boaz represents the principle that restores to the original Unity what has been temporarily separated from it. There has never been any actual separation of Being—the family claim always remained with the property even while it was held by outsiders, otherwise it could never have been reclaimed. But it takes the Love principle to put this claim into active practice.

When this starts to operate with the understanding of its rightful authority to do so, then the individual returns to Unity and recognizes himself as the specific expression of the Universal through his own inherent nature.

These two pillars, therefore, represent the two great spiritual principles that form the foundation of all Life: Jachin symbolizing the Unity that comes from Being, and Boaz symbolizing the Unity that emerges from Love. In this Dual-Unity we discover the key to every conceivable involution or evolution of Spirit; and it is therefore not without good reason that the record of these two ancient pillars has been preserved in our Scriptures. And finally we may regard this as an indication of the character of our Scriptures in general. They contain infinite meanings; and often those passages which appear on the surface to be most meaningless will be found to possess the deepest significance. The Book, which we often read so casually, conceals beneath its sometimes seemingly trivial words the secrets of other things. The twin pillars Jachin and Boaz bear witness to this truth.[5]

The following comment was made by Judge Troward after this paper was published in Expression:

"The Two Pillars of the Universe are Personality and Mathematics, represented by Boaz and Jachin respectively. This represents the most fundamental simplification possible when breaking down all existence. Balance involves maintaining the Equilibrium or Alternating Current between these two Principles. Personality serves as the Absolute Factor. Mathematics functions as the Relative Factor, since it simply Measures various Rates or Scales. Mathematics is absolute in this particular sense. Once a specific scale has been chosen, all its consequences will unfold according to an unforgiving Law of Order and Proportion; however, the choice of the scale and the transition from one scale to another lies entirely within Personality's domain. What Personality cannot accomplish is making one Scale generate the outcomes of another, but it can discard one scale and replace it with a different one. Therefore, Personality encompasses within itself the Universal Scale, and can either adapt itself to lower rates of motion that have already been established, or can elevate them to match its own rate of motion. Thus, Personality stands as the supreme Ultimate Fact in all existence."

"Different personalities should be viewed as varying levels of consciousness. They represent different stages in the emergence of The Power that recognizes Itself."

XXI: Hephzibah

"You will no longer be called Forsaken; your land will no longer be called Desolate. Instead, you will be called Hephzibah, and your land will be called Beulah, because the Lord takes delight in you, and your land will be married" (Isaiah 62:4). The name Hephzibah—or as it could be written, Hafzbah—carries a very specific meaning to anyone who has lived in the East, and brings to mind a series of related words all sharing the same root hafz, which means "guarding" or "taking care of." Examples include hafiz, meaning a protector; muhafiz, meaning a custodian, as seen in the term muhafiz daftar, which refers to a chief record-keeper; or hifazat, meaning custody, as in bahifazat polis, meaning in police custody; or daim-ul-hafz, meaning life imprisonment, along with other similar expressions.

All words from this root convey the concept of "guarding," so the name Haphzibah immediately reveals its own significance. It means "one who is guarded," a "protected one." Corresponding to this, there must be some force that provides protection, and this force is identified in Hosea ii, 16, where it is called "Ishi." "And it shall be at that day, saith the Lord, that thou shalt call me Ishi; and thou shalt call me no more Baali." "Baali" means "lord," "Ishi" means "husband," and between these two terms lies an entire world of difference.

To call the Great Power "Baali" means living in one world, while calling it "Ishi" means living in an entirely different one. The world ruled by Baali is inhabited by "miserable worms of the dust" and other crawling creatures; however, the world warmed and illuminated by "Ishi" is one where men and women stand tall, aware of their own divine nature, rather than scurrying around trying to avoid being trampled under Moloch's feet as he marches through his territories. If the name Baali didn't suggest a false idea, there would be no reason to replace it with another, so this change of name signals the mind's opening to a broader and more accurate understanding of the true nature of the universe's Ruling Principle. It is not a domineering dictator, the ultimate embodiment of self-glorification, bad-tempered and vindictive when its petty vanity isn't satisfied by hearing its own praise formally declared, often from lips moved only by fear; nor is it an all-powerful extortioner seeking to take away what we treasure most, either to feed its greed or to prove its authority. This is the image that people create of God and then bow before it in terror, offering worship that is actually the worship of Baal, and making life empty because all the vitality has been drained from it.

Ishi represents the complete opposite idea—a wise and loving husband rather than a harsh master exploiting his servants. When viewed correctly, the relationship between husband and wife contains no question of who is superior or inferior to the other. It would be like asking whether the front wheel or rear wheel of your bicycle matters more. The two form one complete unit, where both parts serve complementary and equally essential roles; precisely because of this, their functions cannot be the same.

In a well-organized household where husband and wife are bound together by shared love and respect, we observe that the man's role involves engaging with the broader world and supplying his wife with everything necessary for maintaining and ensuring the comfort of their home, while the woman's role centers on managing and distributing what her husband provides, exercising her own judgment in this task; and a wise man, understanding that he can rely on a prudent wife, doesn't feel the need to interfere in every detail. Consequently, everything operates smoothly—the woman freed from duties that don't naturally belong to her, and the man freed from responsibilities that aren't naturally his. However, should any confusion or threat emerge, the woman understands that she will receive from her husband all the direction and protection that the situation demands, given that he is the intelligent and capable man we have assumed him to be, and having this confidence she can continue pursuing the activities within her own domain without being troubled by worries or concerns.

It is this relationship of protection and guidance that the word Hephzibah represents. This is the name given to those who recognize their connection with the all-governing Divine Spirit. Anyone who understands this unity with the Spirit discovers that they are both guided and protected. Here we encounter the edge of a profound natural mystery, which served as the foundation for everything most precious in the advanced mysteries of ancient times, and whose essence we must grasp if we want to make any advancement in the future, regardless of whatever method we might choose to express this concept to ourselves or others. This concerns the relationship between the individual mind and the Universal Mind, the blending of unity with independence which, while completely clear when we understand it through personal experience, is nearly impossible to express in words, but which is often depicted in the Bible through the imagery of marriage relationships.

It is a fundamental principle that permeates all of Nature in various forms and has been represented symbolically in every religion the world has ever known; and to the extent that an individual recognizes this relationship, he will discover that he can utilize the Universal Mind while simultaneously being directed and protected by it. Just imagine what it would mean to possess the power of the Universal Mind without having its guidance. It would be like the ancient tale of Phaeton attempting to drive the chariot of the Sun, which resulted in his own destruction; and unlimited power without proper guidance would be the most terrible curse that anyone could bring upon themselves.

The relationship between the individual mind and the Universal Mind, as shown in the interconnected names of Hephzibah and Ishi, must always be kept in view; for the Great Guiding Mind, though it vastly surpasses our intellectual awareness, is not separate from ourselves. It is The One Self that serves as the foundation for all individual selves, and which is, therefore, in all its boundlessness, as completely united with each person as if no other being existed. Therefore we do not need to look outside ourselves to find it, for it is the infinite expansion of everything we truly are, having, in fact, no room for those negative forms of evil with which we fill a world of illusion, for it is the very Light itself, and within it all illusion is dissolved; but it is the infinite expansion of everything in us that is Positive, everything that is genuinely alive.

Therefore, when we seek guidance and protection, we're not depending on some external power borrowed from outside sources, held at the whim and choice of someone else, but on the fundamental truth of our own nature, which we can direct in any way we choose with complete freedom, knowing no restrictions except the duty not to harm our own purest and highest emotions. And this relationship is completely natural. We must find the right balance between begging and disregarding. A natural law doesn't need to be pleaded with before it will function; and, conversely, we cannot make use of it while ignoring that it exists.

What we need to do, then, is accept how this law works and use it accordingly. Since this is the law of Mind, and Mind is Personality, this Power—which is both ourselves and beyond ourselves—can be approached as a Person and spoken to, with its responses received through the inner ear of the heart. Any philosophical system that doesn't lead to this personal relationship with the Divine Mind misses the point. It might be correct as far as it goes, but it doesn't go far enough and fails to connect us with our essential center. Names matter little as long as the relationship is genuine. The Supreme Mind we communicate with can only be found in the deepest parts of our own being, and, as Tennyson puts it, is more truly ourselves than our own hands and feet. It is our natural foundation; and understanding this, we will discover ourselves to be truly "protected ones," led by the Spirit in all matters, with nothing too significant and nothing too small to fall outside the great Law of our existence.

There is another dimension of the Spirit where it appears as a Power that can be utilized; and the complete flow of life exists in the continuous shift between this dimension and the one we have been examining, yet we remain forever connected to the Universal Mind just as a flower draws life through its roots. This connection is inherent and cannot be broken; however, it must be consciously recognized before it can be consciously employed. All our growth consists of becoming increasingly aware of this connection, which allows us to direct the higher power toward whatever goal we may be pursuing, not simply hoping it might respond, but with absolute certainty that by the law of its own nature it must do so, and similarly with the understanding that by this same law it must also lead us in choosing the right objectives and the right approaches.

Experience teaches us to recognize the warning signals from

our inner guide. A deep-rooted feeling of dissatisfaction, an unexplainable sense that something isn't quite right, are the signs we should pay attention to; for we are protected beings, and these internal warnings come from the deepest part of our nature which is the direct flow of the Great Universal Life into our individual existence. But when we listen to this guidance, we discover ourselves protected, not like prisoners, but like a cherished and respected wife, whose freedom is guaranteed by a protection that prevents any harm from reaching her; we find that the Law of our nature is Liberty, and that only our own lack of understanding can exclude us from it.

XXII: Mind and Hand

I have before me a fascinating piece of ancient Egyptian symbolism. It depicts the sun sending countless rays down to the earth, with the distinctive feature that each ray ends in a hand. This way of representing the sun is so uncommon that it suggests the designer had some idea in mind that differs from those typically associated with the sun as a spiritual symbol; and, if I understand the symbol correctly, it presents the truth, not only of the Divine Being as the Great Source of all Life and all Illumination, but also the related truth of our individual connection to that center. Each ray ends with a hand, and a hand symbolizes active work; and I believe it would be hard to find a better symbolic representation of countless individualities, each working independently, yet all drawing their activity from a shared source. The hand works upon the earth, and the sun, from which it extends as a ray, shines in the heavens; but the connecting line reveals where all the strength and skill of the hand come from.

If we examine the small-scale world of our own being, we discover this same principle perfectly reflected. Our hand serves as the tool through which all our work gets accomplished—whether it's writing, creating art, building things, or managing household tasks—but we understand that all this work is actually the work of the mind, the willpower at the core of our system, which first decides what needs to be done, and then directs the hand to carry it out; and in performing this work the mind and hand unite as one, so that the hand becomes nothing other than the mind in action. Now, when we apply this comparison to the larger universe, we can see that each of us occupies the same relationship to the Universal Mind that our hand has to our individual mind—at least, that represents our natural relationship; and we will never express our complete power unless we operate from this perspective.

We correctly recognize our will as the center of our individuality, but we would do better to imagine our individuality as an ellipse rather than a circle—a shape that has two "conjugate foci," two balanced centers of revolution instead of just one. One of these centers is our willpower or ability to act, and the other is our consciousness or awareness of existence. If we only develop one of these two centers, we will lose both our mental and moral balance. If we lose sight of the center that represents our personal will, we will become weak dreamers without any strength of character. And if, in our eagerness to develop strength of character, we lose sight of the other center, we will discover that we have lost what corresponds to the lungs and heart in our physical body. Our backbone, no matter how perfectly developed, will rapidly wither away from lack of those functions that provide vitality to the entire system, and will only be suitable for display in a museum to demonstrate what a rigid, lifeless thing the strongest spinal column becomes when separated from the living system that alone can nourish it. We must recognize one focus of our individuality as clearly as the other, and bring both into equal balance, if we want to develop all our abilities and rise to that perfection of Life which has no limits to its magnificent possibilities.

Using the ancient Egyptian symbol mentioned earlier, and thinking of ourselves as the hand, we discover that all our power comes from an infinite center. Since this center is infinite, we never need to worry that we'll fail to attract everything we need for our work—whether that's the wisdom to grasp the right tool or the strength to use it effectively. Furthermore, the symbol teaches us that this central power is universal in nature. This represents a crucial truth. It serves as the center from which all hands emerge, and it remains equally accessible to every single hand. Each hand performs its individual task, and the entire central energy is available for its specific purpose. The role of the central energy itself is to provide life force to the hands, and it's the hands that transform this universal power into all the different forms of application that their various abilities and circumstances make possible. We, as the hands, exist and function because the Central Mind exists and functions within us. We are united with it, and it is united with us. As long as we maintain this fundamental truth in our awareness, we recognize ourselves as beings of boundless goodness, intelligence, and power, and we operate with complete strength and confidence. However, if we lose sight of this truth, we'll discover that even the strongest willpower must eventually become depleted in the uneven battle of the individual against the universe.

For if we don't recognize the Central Mind as the source of our vitality, we are literally "fighting for our own hand," and all the other hands are against us, because we have lost the principle of connection with them. This is what must inevitably happen if we rely on nothing but our individual willpower. But if we realize that the will is the power by which we give out, and that every giving out implies a corresponding taking in, then we shall find in the boundless ocean of central living Spirit the source from which we can go on taking in infinitely, and which thus enables us to give out to any extent we choose. But for wise and effective giving out a strong and enlightened will is an absolute necessity, and therefore we do well to cultivate the will, or the active side of our nature. But we must equally cultivate the receptive side as well; and when we do this correctly by seeing in the Infinite Mind the one source of supply, our willpower becomes intensified by the knowledge that the whole power of the Infinite is present to support it; and with this continual sense of Infinite Power behind us we can go calmly and steadily to the accomplishment of any purpose, however difficult, without strain or effort, knowing that it shall be achieved, not by the hand alone, but by the invincible Mind that works through it. "Not by might, nor by power, but by My Spirit, saith the Lord of hosts."

XXIII: The Central Control

When we think about the relationships between body, soul, and spirit, and between the Universal Mind and individual mind—the systematic study of which forms Mental Science—we must always remember that these relationships show unity, not separation, among these principles. We need to learn not to assign one aspect of our actions to one part of our being and another aspect to a different part. Neither our actions nor our functions are divided into separate components. Our action forms a complete whole, and the being performing it is also a complete whole, and in a healthy system the interactive movements of these principles work so harmoniously that they only create the feeling of a perfectly whole and unified self. If we experience any other feeling, we can be certain that something is functioning abnormally somewhere, and we should work to identify and eliminate whatever is causing it. This happens because in any perfect system there can only be one center of control.

A conflict between controlling principles would destroy the organic wholeness; either the elements would split apart and cluster around one center or another based on their natural connections, creating two separate identities, or they would fall into complete chaotic disorder. In both situations, the original organism would stop existing. Looking at it this way, it becomes obvious that if we want to keep our individuality—in other words, if we want to continue existing—we can only do so by maintaining our grip on the central controlling principle within ourselves. If this is the foundation of our existence, then all our future growth depends on recognizing and embracing this central controlling principle. All our efforts should focus on this goal; otherwise, our studies in Mental Science will only lead us into a confusing maze of principles and opposing principles, which will be much worse than the state of innocent simplicity we began with.

The Will serves as this central controlling principle, and we must always remember that all the other principles we've studied exist solely as its tools. The Will represents our true self, with all other elements functioning as its expressions, and our entire development involves increasingly recognizing this truth. The Will declares "I AM," and therefore, no matter how elevated or seemingly miraculous our abilities may become in their advanced forms, they all remain under the central governing power of the Will. When the enlightened Will learns to perfectly align itself with the unlimited powers of knowledge, judgment, and creative thought available to it, the individual will achieve complete wholeness, and all limitations will disappear forever.

And nothing less than this awareness of Perfect Wholeness can truly fulfill us. Anything that falls short of this represents, to that extent, an expression of the principle of Death—that great adversary against which the principle of Life must continue to fight an endless battle, in whatever form or degree it may appear, until "death is swallowed up in victory." There can be no middle ground. Either we are affirming Life as a principle, or we are denying it, regardless of whether on a large or small scale; and the standard by which we determine our stance is our recognition of our own Wholeness. Death represents the principle of breakdown; and whenever we acknowledge the power of any part of our being, whether spiritual or physical, to create any condition independent of the Will's intention, we acknowledge that the force of breakdown is stronger than the controlling center within ourselves, and we think of ourselves as being held captive by an enemy, from which captivity the only path to freedom is through achieving a more accurate way of thinking.

The reason for this is that we have given up our controlling position over the entire system, either through lack of knowledge or through neglect, and we have lost the element of Purpose, which must always be the center around which our sense of individuality revolves. Every state of our consciousness, whether we are actively engaged or passively receiving, should result from a clear purpose that we have chosen through our own free will; the passive states should be just as much under the control of our Will as the active ones. It is this absence of purpose that strips us of our power. The higher and more clearly we define our purpose, the greater motivation we have for developing our control over all our abilities to achieve it; and since the most magnificent of all purposes is the strengthening and elevating of Life, to the extent that we make this our goal we will discover ourselves in harmony with the Supreme Universal Mind, each of us working within our individual sphere to advance the same purpose that drives the governing principle of the Great Whole, and as a result, we will find that its intelligence and powers are available to us.

But in all of this, there should be no strain. The genuine practice of the Will isn't about applying unnatural force. It's simply about directing our abilities into their natural pathways by intelligently recognizing which direction those pathways lead. Though they may vary in specifics, they share one clearly defined common direction toward increasing Life—whether within ourselves or in others—and if we maintain this focus consistently, all our abilities, both internal and external, will work together so harmoniously that no single one of them will seem to act independently. The distinctions we make for learning purposes will be set aside, and the Self within us will prove to be the fulfillment of a magnificent ideal being, simultaneously individual and universal, consciously free in its individual completeness and in its joyful participation in the Life of the Universal Whole.

XXIV: What Is Higher Thought?

Resolution passed in October 1902 by the Kensington Higher Thought Centre.

"That the Centre represents the clear teaching of the complete unity between Creator and Creation—Cause and Effect—and that nothing that might contradict or oppose these principles will be allowed on the 'Higher Thought' Centre Platform."

"By Oneness of Cause and Effect is meant that the Effect (man) consists only of what the Cause is; however, a part (individual personality) is not therefore equal in scope to the whole."

This decision is extremely important. The moment you accept that any power exists outside yourself, no matter how kind you might think it is, you plant a seed that will eventually grow into

"Fear," which completely destroys Life, Love, and Liberty. There's no middle ground here. If we say we're merely reflections of The Life, even perfect ones, we've already given up our birthright in making that admission. No matter how tiny or reasonable the thought might seem that suggests we're anything less in essence than The Life Itself, it will eventually grow and destroy the Life-Principle completely. We are It itself. The only difference is like that between the general category and the specific example of the same thing. We must fight passionately, both inside ourselves and in the world around us, for this one great foundation and never, from now until forever, allow even for a moment any thought that goes against this Basic Truth of Being.

The main ideas associated with Higher Thought are (I) That humans control their circumstances, rather than being controlled by them, and (II) as a result of the previous point, that anything which teaches us to depend on power borrowed from a source outside ourselves is not Higher Thought; and that anything which explains to us the infinite source of our own inherent power and the resulting unlimited nature of that power is Higher Thought. This prevents the use of terms which may only confuse those not familiar with abstract language, and is essentially the same as the resolution of October, 1902.

THE END

Thank You For Reading

You've Just Read a Piece of the Greatest Library Ever Rebuilt

Thank you for reading.

This book is one of thousands we're restoring, reimagining, and translating as part of the **Modern Library of Alexandria** — a global movement to preserve and share humanity's most important ideas.

What was once lost to fire and time is now rising again — not just as memory, but as living, breathing knowledge, freely accessible to all.

What You Can Do Next:

- **Keep Reading.**

  Discover more legendary works — in beautiful print, audiobook, or digital form — at LibraryofAlexandria.com.

- **Build Your Own Library.**

  Every title is available as a paperback, hardcover, or collectible boxset — at true printing cost. Craft a personal library worthy of display.

- **Spread the Light.**

  Share this book. Tell others about the movement. Help us translate every timeless work into every language, so no reader is ever left behind.

By finishing this book, you've already taken part in something extraordinary.

Join us at LibraryofAlexandria.com

Together, we're rebuilding the greatest library the world has ever known.

With appreciation,

The Modern Library of Alexandria Team

Visit:
www.libraryofalexandria.com
Or scan the code below: